A MISTLETOE KISS
WITH THE BOSS

A MISTLETOE KISS WITH THE BOSS

BY

SUSAN MEIER

MILLS & BOON

First published in Great Britain 2016
By Mills & Boon, an imprint of HarperCollins*Publishers*
1 London Bridge Street, London, SE1 9GF

Large Print edition 2017

© 2016 Linda Susan Meier

ISBN: 978-0-263-07061-3

Printed and bound in Great Britain
by CPI Antony Rowe, Chippenham, Wiltshire

CHAPTER ONE

WHEN THE ELEVATOR bell rang in the lobby of the upscale Paris hotel, Kristen Anderson's heart thumped. She spun to face the ornate wrought iron doors, her whole body shivering in anticipation—

Two middle-aged American women got out.

She didn't have time to sag with disappointment, because someone tapped her on the shoulder and asked her a quiet question.

In French.

Which she didn't speak.

She turned around to see a man dressed in a suit, undoubtedly the desk clerk.

Speaking English, because her native Grennadian was nearly unheard of, she said, "I'm sorry. I don't speak French."

The elevator bell dinged again. Her head snapped toward the sound.

In perfect English, the desk clerk said, "May I ask, mademoiselle, your business in our hotel?"

She pointed at the tall, broad man exiting the elevator. "I want to see him."

She took two steps toward Dean Suminski, chairman of the board and CEO of Suminski Stuff, but the clerk caught her arm.

"No, mademoiselle." He shook his finger like a metronome. "You will not disturb a guest."

Walking toward her, Dean Suminski shrugged into a gorgeous charcoal-gray overcoat. His eyes were down. She guessed that was his way of ignoring anyone who might be around him. But she didn't care. Getting him to visit Grennady and consider it as the place to relocate his company was her mission for her country. Approaching him was also practice for when she had to deal with men like him on a daily basis after she started her charitable foundation. One desk clerk wouldn't stop her.

"Sorry, Pierre." She pulled her arm out of his short, stubby fingers. "Someday I'm going to build schools in third world countries. I have to learn to be brash."

She spun away from the clerk and shouted, "Mr. Suminski!"

He totally ignored her.

"Mr. Suminski! I know that's you. I've seen your face on the internet."

He walked to the door.

She scurried after him. "I just need two minutes."

Out of the corner of her eye, she saw the clerk point at a man behind another discreet desk. He nodded and bounded toward her. But Suminski walked out the door and she stayed on his heels, catching him when he stopped in front of a limo.

"Seriously. Two minutes. That's all I need."

In the silence of the crisp early December morning, at a hotel set back, away from the congestion of Paris's main thoroughfare, she heard his annoyed sigh and was surprised when he faced her.

"Who are you?"

With his dark eyes locked on her face, Kristen froze. His black hair was perfect, not a strand out of place. His high forehead, straight nose and high cheekbones could have made him a king.

When she didn't answer, he said, "Fine," and began to turn away.

"I'm Kristen Anderson," she said, her voice coming out louder than it should. She sucked in a quick gulp of air and calmed herself. When she spoke again, it was quieter, smoother, and with authority. "Gennady would like you to consider moving your company to our country."

He faced her again. "Prince Alex would know I wasn't interested."

Prince Alex was the husband of Kristen's boss, Princess Eva. As executive assistant to Gennady's future queen, Kristen knew Alex had immediately said no to considering Suminski Stuff as one of the tech companies being recruited to boost their flagging economy. But their options had run out. Dean's was the only company left.

"So that's why you weren't put on the list?"

He smiled. But the movement wasn't warm or friendly. More sarcastic. Almost frightening. "There's a list?"

"There was. It's dwindled."

"To no one, I'm guessing, if they sent you to barge in on my day."

She swallowed. Those black eyes were just too intense—like they saw every damned thing going on in her head. She'd read that he was shrewd, uncanny in his ability to judge his opponents. Orphaned at four, raised by a cold grandmother who hadn't wanted him, he'd played video games to amuse himself. At fourteen, he'd gone to business school because he'd taught himself to code and didn't need any more instructions in computers. He was brilliant. He was arrogant. He was also their last chance.

She opened her hands in supplication. "If you could give me two minutes of your time, I could persuade you to visit and make an assessment about whether or not you might consider, perhaps, moving your company to Grennady."

"That's a lotta maybes and mights and perhapses."

"It's possible you're not looking to move."

"I'm not."

"You should be. Grennady is a beautiful country with a diverse labor pool."

He scowled, and really just scared the hell out of her. Tall, broad-shouldered, and blunt, he made her blood tingle with fear. And she had the feeling he did it deliberately. Maybe this was why Prince Alex didn't want him in their country? And maybe she had overstepped in contacting him. Grennady might be desperate to find an employer who could keep their younger, educated residents at home, but Suminski Stuff wasn't the answer.

She stepped back. "You know what? I'm sorry I bothered you. Have a nice day."

He shook his head. "You're gonna give up that easily? I had higher hopes for you."

Her face scrunched in confusion. "What?"

"You obviously flew from your frozen country to Paris where you don't even speak the language." His head tilted. "I heard you tell the clerk. You also didn't mind running after me, shouting in a quiet lobby. That takes some guts. But when you finally had my attention, you backed off." He almost smiled. "Too bad."

He turned to leave, but she caught his arm. "What would you have done, if you were me?"

He laughed. "So now you want me to teach you how to dicker?"

His dark eyes held her gaze. She swallowed down her fear because, damn it, why should she be afraid of this guy just because he had money? And was big. And handsome. And had a terrifying way of looking at her.

"I don't want you to teach me to dicker. I want you to listen to my pitch for about fifteen minutes."

"Before you said two minutes."

"That was if I didn't show you some pictures."

He looked at the blue sky, then back at her. "All right. Get in the car. I'm on my way to the airport. You've got the entire drive. Give it your best shot."

Hope burst inside her. Maybe he wasn't so bad, after all? "Really?"

He motioned to the black limo awaiting him. "Here's lesson one. Don't question good luck."

The driver opened the car door and Kristen slid inside. Warm leather seats arranged in a semicircle greeted her.

Dean Suminski eased in beside her. A few seconds passed in silence as the driver got behind the wheel. Dean spent the time texting.

As the car pulled away from the hotel, Kristen said, "So I'm assuming you already know a little bit about Grennady?"

"I own controlling interest in a big company. I know who's managing the world's oil. I met Xaviera's Prince Alex a few years back. When he married, I did my research."

"Why would you care who he married?"

He sniffed a laugh. "Would you put your money in oil stocks if the region was unstable?"

"That has nothing to do with Alex getting married. Besides, that region's always unstable."

"Let's call it controlled instability because of people like Prince Alex's dad, King Ronaldo. As long as Ronaldo is happy, he's strong. I needed to make sure Alex's marriage didn't rock the boat."

She supposed that was true. "So you know that our country's every bit as well ruled as Xaviera."

"Your country nearly had a coup at the beginning of the year."

"Nearly. King Mason was on top of things."

He made a noncommittal sound.

"But, just for the sake of argument, let's pretend he wasn't. He is now."

"True."

"We're going through something that could be described as a renaissance, and you could be part of that."

"I'm rich. I don't need to be part of anything."

His phone rang. He slid it from his breast pocket. "Very few people have this number. So if someone's calling it's important." He clicked the button to answer. "Hello?"

A pause.

"Maurice! Je m'excuse. Mon voyage a été coupé court..."

French again. Damn it. She knew two languages. The language of her country and English. It was becoming clear that she would have to fix that, if she wanted to run an international charity.

As he went on, holding a conversation in a language she didn't speak, she looked at the luxurious interior of the car. She'd ridden in limos with the princess, of course, but this felt different. She wasn't the scampering, scrambling employee of an important person, doing her job to make Eva's life easier. She was the one talking to the important person.

She was more than getting her feet wet with this guy. He took her seriously.

She felt herself making her first shaky step into the life and work she really wanted. Though she loved being Princess Eva's assistant, she had a degree in economics and a plan to change the world. When she was in high school, her pen pal Aasera had been one of six kids, living in Iraq. Her brothers had been educated, but she and her sisters were not. So she'd sneaked her brothers' books. When they discovered, she'd begged them to teach her to read and write, and they did.

She had been brave, determined. She'd often said her country would be a different place if women were educated, and she'd intended to make that happen. But she'd been killed by a suicide bomber, and in her grief Kristen had vowed to make Aasera's wish a reality.

Today, she was finally beginning to feel she could make that happen.

Dean hung up the phone. "Sorry about that."

"It's fine."

The words were barely out of her mouth before his phone rang again.

He waved it at her. "Sorry. I have to answer."

This time he spoke fluent Spanish. Not wanting to appear to be listening in, though she couldn't since she also didn't speak Spanish, she looked at the beauty of Paris outside the car windows. The curved arches. The ornate buildings. Happy people bundled in scarves and warm coats, sitting on the chairs of sidewalk cafes, in spite of the December cold.

She almost couldn't believe she'd been courageous enough to take her own money and track down Dean Suminski, but here she was, in Paris, trying to influence him as an equal—or at least as someone who deserved his support. It filled her chest with pride and her stomach with butterflies, but after three years as Eva's assistant, she was ready to move on.

Dean talked so long that the city gave way to a quieter area, and then the buildings became fewer and farther apart. Suddenly a private airstrip appeared. Eight or ten bright blue, gray and tan metal hangars gleamed in the morning sun. Around them were five jets that ranged from a sleek, slim, small one to a plane big enough to hold the entirety of Grennady's parliament.

Dean Suminski continued talking as the limo stopped in front of one of the smaller, sleeker jets. He talked as the driver opened his door. He talked as he motioned for her to get out of the limo and as he followed her out and onto the tarmac.

Finally, he clicked off the call. "This wasn't my fault. As I said, any call that comes in on this phone is important. Normally, I don't feel the need to make amends, but if you want, you can fly to New York with me. That gives you almost nine hours to make your pitch."

Her eyes bulged. It was one thing to take a few steps toward her dreams, quite another to cross an ocean. "Fly to New York?"

"You don't have time?"

"I…" She didn't want to tell him she'd used her own money to travel to Paris and couldn't miss her flight home the following morning. She didn't want to tell him that her boss and her husband were at Prince Alex's island home of Xaviera with his family, at the end of their vacation celebrating American Thanksgiving with Princess Ginny and Queen Rose. She didn't want to admit that Princess Eva didn't know where Kristen was, and hadn't authorized her talking to him. She wanted to surprise them with a visit from Dean Suminski in January, as a way to thank them for being so good to her, but also to show them she could get a job done. So that when she left their employ to begin her charity, they'd be her first backers.

But she was also proving to herself she had what it took to be more than an executive assistant. If she couldn't persuade Dean Suminski to visit Grennady with an eye toward relocating, would she be able to persuade benefactors to put up the millions of dollars she would need for her schools?

"Once we get to New York, the plane will turn around and bring you back home."

Probably in time for her flight. Or she could simply tell Dean Suminski to instruct the pilot to take her back to Grennady. "That's generous."

His eyes turned down at the corners as he frowned. "Generous?"

"Well, you could leave me at the airport."

"I could." He glanced away, then looked back. "I know I have a reputation for being…well, not a nice guy. But you don't need me to be a nice guy. You want time to make a pitch. I'm offering it. Consider this an early Christmas present."

It suddenly struck her that he must be interested. He hadn't told her to get lost at the hotel. He'd offered her time in his limo, though that hadn't worked out. But here he was again, giving her a chance to sell him on her country.

"Thought you said you weren't thinking of relocating?"

"Thought you said I should be."

CHAPTER TWO

"You should."

Dean Suminski studied the pretty girl in front of him. Blonde with pale green eyes and a generous mouth made for kissing, she wore a simple black wool coat over black pants and sensible shoes. Normally, he would have had his bodyguard deal with anyone who approached him, but she reminded him of himself ten years ago, when Suminski Stuff was in its infancy. When he wore simple, practical clothes, hoping he didn't stand out for his lack of sophistication, and when he was trying to raise money from investors to start his business.

Still, he hadn't gotten this far by being stupid. He'd texted his executive assistant and told her to get everything she could on Kristen Anderson of Grennady, and that's what the call in

Spanish had been about. This woman really did work for Princess Eva.

If Grennady's royal family had sent her to him, there was a reason. He might not want to be part of a renaissance precipitated by a near coup, but he wouldn't mind having a desperate country at his mercy.

He said, "All right. I'll admit that the most popular places to locate a corporation in the United States are getting crowded." He speared her with a look, delving deeply into those pretty green eyes, knowing she wasn't very experienced at negotiating and wondering why a princess would send *her*. Surely, more astute negotiators or even public relations people would do a better job.

Especially since he knew Alex Sancho, Princess Eva's husband, didn't like him.

Her eyes brightened. "So there is a chance you'd relocate?"

The sparkle in her eyes hit him like a punch to the gut, surprising him. Those soft green orbs were little mirrors to her happy soul. And that lush, kiss-me mouth? It took a stronger man than he was not to notice its plump fullness.

Still, he shouldn't be looking. He only dated sophisticates. Women who took lovers, who weren't seeking happily-ever-after, as this bubbly, obviously naïve woman would be.

But the feeling in his gut wouldn't go away. It kept telling him that something about her was important. And he should pay attention.

He pointed at the plane. "Let's not get ahead of ourselves."

She preceded him up the short stack of steps into his jet. When she gasped, he laughed.

"The princess never takes you on her jet?"

"Up until last year, she didn't do much government business. Actually, she didn't even have bodyguards."

He raised his eyebrows. "Are you going to waste these next few hours gossiping?"

"No." She waved her hands. "Sorry. I know your time is precious."

"Let's just buckle in and you can start your pitch once we're at cruising altitude."

As he spoke, his second-in-command and best friend, Jason Wilson, stepped into the corridor from the office in the back.

Short, twenty or thirty pounds overweight, but looking expensive and self-assured in his three-piece suit, Jason said, "We have a problem."

Dean motioned for Kristen to take a seat and buckle in. "I suppose we do if you flew the whole way to Europe rather than phone me."

Jason caught Dean's arm and moved him to the back of the plane before he whispered, "While you were in meetings yesterday, I got word from a few investment firms that our stock's about to be downgraded and they're going to advise investors to sell."

Forgetting all about Kristen Anderson, he gaped at Jason. *"Sell?"*

"*Tech Junkie* ran an article about you. They suggested that the new product is late because we don't have one."

"That's absurd!"

"Oh, it gets worse. They said you're so far removed from real life and so far removed from real people that it's a miracle you came up with the original operating system and games that you did. They claim being out of touch with real people means you can't figure out what they want because you're not one of them."

"How I live has nothing to do with my abilities."

"Not according to the pundits quoted in the article. They say your reign is over. That you had five or six good ideas and exhausted them."

The urge to shake his head at the stupidity of some people was nearly overwhelming. He was a genius, for crying out loud. Of course he didn't live like a normal person.

"I spent my childhood poor, looking for ways to entertain myself. I know software. I know games."

"They say that's what got you here. But your ideas are gone."

He tossed his hands in frustration. "We have a fantastic series of games in the works!"

"In the works for three years. Too long in this market." Jason snapped his fingers. "Everything's all about speed these days."

"The series has to be perfect before I can even talk about it, let alone roll it out."

"Then you're pretty much screwed." Jason's gaze strayed to Kristen. "Who's that?"

He didn't like explaining himself to anybody. Not even his best friend—especially since he wasn't entirely clear why he was willing to hear Kristen Anderson's pitch. Every time he looked at her, he got a "there's an opportunity here" feeling. Which made no sense since Alex Sancho was married to her boss. Couple that with the way he kept noticing all the wrong things about her, and being around her was tempting fate. Which was absurd. He did not tempt fate, push envelopes or even take risks. He was cautious. That's why he was rich.

Yet here she was in his jet.

He held back a wince as he said, "She's a girl I met at the hotel."

Jason's eyes widened. "Really?"

Deciding to let honest and genuine Kristen explain this, he turned and started up the aisle to the four plush seats. "Kristen, this is Jason Wilson, my second in command."

Kristen jumped off her seat and extended her

hand. "Kristen Anderson. I work for Princess Eva of Grennady."

Jason's gaze walked back to Dean. *"Prince Alex's wife's assistant* is your new girlfriend?"

She laughed. "No. I'm not his girlfriend. My country wants your company to consider relocating to Grennady."

The pilot's voice came over the speaker, advising passengers to buckle seat belts and get ready for takeoff.

Dean caught the gaze of Kristen's happy green eyes. An unwanted tingle of attraction zipped through him, but so did that damned feeling that she, somehow, was important.

He said, "You buckle in," then he faced Jason. "Let's take this discussion to the office."

He followed his friend down the aisle to the compact room. As they fastened their seat belts, Jason said, "So, who is she really?"

Dean focused his attention on his cantankerous buckle so he didn't have to look at Jason. "She told you. She's from Grennady. Her country wants us to consider locating there."

Jason's eyes narrowed. "You don't *like* her?"

He did actually. Even if he paid no attention to the "she's important somehow" feeling or the way her physical appearance kept tempting him, she was smart and ambitious. She was also totally inexperienced, but that might be why she was such a curiosity. She wasn't a shark. She wasn't a schmoozer. She was too naïve, clearly too green to be either of those. She was just a woman trying to do a job. If the royal family had an agenda in sending her, he didn't think she knew it.

"If you're asking if I want to take her out, the answer is no." He might be attracted to her, but he didn't date. And she was too naïve to fit the role as his lover. "I told her I'd listen to her pitch in the car, but got caught up in a phone conversation with Stella. So I told her I'd listen on the plane. When we land in New York, the plane will turn around and take her home."

Jason said, "Okay, fine," as the jet taxied. "As long as this mess with investors comes first."

"Of course."

When they were in the air, climbing to cruising altitude, he and Jason began a discussion of how to combat the *Tech Junkie* article. But in hours and hours of studying schematics, employee reports and his own damned business plan—which was shot to hell because the schedule was now almost two years behind—all they could come up with was a stopgap measure: contact the most influential brokerage firms and ask them to delay advising their clients to sell to give Suminski Stuff time to get the games to one more set of beta testers.

They made a list of firms to call when they got to New York, and created a script of what they would say, but Dean knew brokers were right to be concerned. The games they'd been working on had had one setback after another because the series was too ambitious. No one really knew how far away it was from rollout. The staff had gotten tired, worn down, and everything was now taking longer than it should.

He'd been warned. But he'd gotten arrogant. *His* staff could do anything...

Or so he'd thought. And now they were in trouble because he couldn't even give a hard date for when it would be ready for another round of beta testing, let alone a hard date for when it would be for sale.

When the script was ready, Jason scrubbed his hand across his mouth. "So this is what we say?"

Dean shrugged, then leaned back in his comfortable chair. "Yes. If the brokers listen to us, I think we'll buy about six weeks. But we're going to have to do some hand-holding. And at the end of that six weeks, we have to have something—even if it's only a date for when it can go into beta testing again."

"Christmas is smack-dab in the middle of those six weeks. Then New Year's."

"So we'll cancel Christmas."

Jason laughed. "We can't cancel a holiday."

"No, but we can cancel vacations and leave."

"They'll hate you."

"Yeah, well, I'm not feeling warm and fuzzy toward them right now, either. Three years they've been working on this. If anybody's got a right to be disappointed, it's me."

The pilot announced that it was time to buckle in for landing and Dean wasn't surprised. The flight to New York had felt like the shortest of his life because he'd spent it figuring out how to keep investors from dumping his stock, when, really, if he was one of them he'd drop his stock like a hot rock.

He and Jason buckled in. The jet landed and taxied to his private hangar. They unbuckled their seat belts and stepped into the aisle only to find Kristen Anderson facing them, looking furious.

He squeezed his eyes shut. *This* was why he didn't deal with people. He wasn't considerate. He had a one-track mind. Right now his company was in danger of total failure. He didn't have time to listen to a pitch for something he neither needed nor wanted.

"Sorry. I'd say you could have the limo ride to my office to chat, but then you wouldn't be able to turn around and fly home."

Her pretty face softened a bit. "I'm okay with that. Just have your plane take me back to Grennady instead of Paris and I'll be fine."

Dean started to say, "Okay," but Jason caught his arm. "She can't have the limo ride. You have to start making those calls the minute we step off this plane. I'm guessing you'll be spending the entire day talking. After that there's the Christmas gala."

"I can miss that."

Jason sniffed a laugh. "Really? After you spend an entire day convincing brokers that the company's solvent and you're fine, not some prima donna genius who doesn't understand real life, you think you can miss an event where you actually mingle like a normal person? The one that opens the season? The one that *everybody* goes to?"

Damn it. Jason was right. The speculation of why he hadn't attended the party of the year could undo all the hours he'd spend making those telephone calls.

He unhappily caught Kristen's gaze. He hated messing up the way he had with her. He didn't make mistakes. And even when he did, somehow or another, the situation turned out okay, as if his instincts could see the future and know there was a reason he'd done whatever unusual thing he'd done.

But not this time.

There was no "reason" that he'd strung her along except that he had an odd feeling in his gut every time he looked at her. And now he had to brush her off.

"I'm sorry, Ms. Anderson. It appears I really don't have time to talk to you. It's best you take the plane back."

"Seriously? I just sat patiently for *hours* and you won't even listen for fifteen minutes?"

The word *sorry* was on the tip of his tongue again but he swallowed it. Technically this wasn't his fault. "You orchestrated this. I told you I was a busy man. You took a risk and it didn't work out."

Jason caught his arm, but he addressed Kristen. "Just hold on for one second." Then he faced Dean. "Can I talk to you in the back?"

Dean reluctantly followed Jason to the aisle in front of the office.

"We sort of have a weird opportunity here."

Not following how or why, Dean said nothing.

"We want to counteract that article. We want brokers and big investors to see you as a normal guy, and be comfortable that you're not worried about the situation with the new games."

Dean quietly said, "Yes."

Jason nudged his head toward the front of the plane. "So why not take her to the party tonight?"

Dean laughed. "What?"

"No one's ever seen you date. You keep your relationships private. The press has been dying to catch you with a woman. But more than that, a date makes you look normal. Happy even. Who knows? The next article might come out speculating that the rollout is late because you're preoccupied with your new girlfriend. It's a chance to totally spin this mess in our favor."

Dean glanced up at Kristen. His heartbeat slowed. The sweet tingle of attraction rolled through him. Attending a party with her was exactly what his hormones wanted. "She is pretty."

"She's more than pretty, Dean. She's gorgeous. The kind of girl everybody expects you to end up with. She, personally, might not have breeding, but she works for a royal family. She's on the periphery of the jet-set crowd, good-looking enough to attract someone like you. The connection is logical. We'll send her out with Stella to get something for the party. Shoes, dress, whatever the hell she needs. Then she's on your arm tonight."

"I'll have to listen to her pitch. Right now," Dean said emphatically. "I'm not stringing her along and I'm not going to let her think I'm using her."

Jason shook his head. "Your honesty is going to bite you in the butt one of these days."

"Yeah, but my arrogance will save me."

Jason slapped his back. "Whatever."

Dean led Jason to the front of the plane. "I'm going to listen to your pitch right now."

Her eyes widened. "You are?"

"Yes. But then I'd like to hire you to do something for me."

"Hire me?"

"Yes." Though he and Jason hadn't discussed paying her, with all the strange feelings tumbling through him when he was around her, he needed to make sure they kept this "date" in perspective. He also wouldn't ask Kristen Anderson to go to the party with him as a favor. Favors implied that he'd be indebted to her. He was indebted to no one. "I'll pay you a hundred thousand dollars to go to a party with me tonight."

She laughed.

He waited until she realized he was serious.

Wide-eyed, she asked, "Why would you do that?"

"You heard a bit of the discussion about my company hitting a bumpy patch?"

She inclined her head in acknowledgment.

"Well, I believe it will make me look a little more—" He wouldn't say "normal." Refused. Being a genius took him out of the normal column, but that didn't mean he didn't understand kids. Especially lonely kids. He had been one. He knew how to entertain them. "—approachable if I go to tonight's gala happy. Having a date will make it appear that everything's fine."

She just looked at him.

"Stocks are funny things," Jason said. "They sometimes rise and fall on rumors. How a company's leader is perceived dictates how much money people are willing to risk."

Dean frowned at Jason. "She has a degree in economics. I'm pretty sure she knows that." He faced Kristen. "What I really need to counter-act that article is for people to perceive me as a regular guy. Dating is something a regular guy does."

"And if I say no, you won't listen to my pitch?"

The odd feeling rolled through him again. The feeling that something about her was significant. Holding the gaze of her pretty eyes, which were serious this time, he knew he had to be fair with her.

"No. Regardless of whether you go to the party with me or not, I'll listen to your pitch. But if you decide to come with me, we'll make arrangements to get you something suitable to wear, and we'll put you up in a hotel suite. Party's not until eight. You can get some sleep so you'll be fresh and happy for tonight. Then tomorrow you're back on this plane, on your way home."

"For a hundred thousand dollars?"

"I'm not paying you more than a hundred thou-sand dollars for a date."

"I don't want more. In fact, I, personally, do not want the money. But I am in the beginning stages of setting up a charity that will build schools in third world countries. I think what I'd really like is a commitment from you to put computers in those schools."

Disappointment flooded him. Just like everybody else, she wanted something from him. She might be on an assignment from Princess Eva and Prince Alex, but *she* had an agenda too. There was nothing special about her.

Still, he was accustomed to people wanting something. Everybody in his life wanted money or a favor or a recommendation of some sort. So what if she was no different? He didn't know why something about her had caught his attention. Maybe hormones mixing with jet lag? Disappointed or not, he was accustomed to this.

"When will the schools be built?"

She bit her lip. "I don't know. I'm in the planning stages of the charity itself. I don't really know when I'll have an actual school."

Jason touched Dean's arm to prevent him from

replying. "So what you want is a promise in writing—"

"An agreement. I want this to be a normal charitable contribution. Not money given to me personally. But a charitable contribution."

Dean nodded. "Okay, we'll write an agreement that states I will put the first three hundred computers in your soon-to-be-developed schools."

"Yes."

He held out his hand to shake hers. "Deal."

She took his hand. "Deal."

CHAPTER THREE

STELLA TURNED OUT to be a thirtysomething hipster with short hair and big glasses, a long sweater over black leggings and tall boots. Standing in the middle of a huge dressing room in an exclusive boutique, Kristen watched Dean's assistant frown at the red dress she'd asked the shop manager to bring in her size.

"Sweetie," she said, then took a sip of her designer coffee. "If I were you, I'd get a black gown. Something I could wear again and again. When you've got a rich man footing the bill, you shop smart."

The boutique manager rolled her eyes.

Kristen winced. "I just want something acceptable. I don't want to break the bank."

Stella sniffed. "Dean Suminski's bank can't be broken." She motioned Kristen back into the curtained-off section of the dressing room. "Try the black one I picked out."

Kristen stepped between the two colorful strips of fabric that blocked off the changing area. When the boutique manager arrived with the black dress, she shrugged out of the cute red gown and into the elegant black one.

"Oh."

She hadn't meant to comment, but the tiny squeak had slipped out. Black satin, sleeveless and formfitting from her chin to her hip bones, the dress flared out from thigh to floor and made a beautiful swishing sound when she moved.

The boutique manager, Jennifer, sighed. "I hate to call that little twit out there right, but this dress is perfect."

They found black shoes of an appropriate height, so the dress wouldn't need to be hemmed, and stunning white-gold earrings and necklace that sparkled against the simplicity of the dress. Then Stella had Dean's driver take them to a hotel on Broadway, where she was led to a suite.

"Get a nap," Stella said. "I'll be in the front room when your dress and shoes are delivered.

I'll arrange for a hairstylist and someone to do your makeup."

"I have makeup in my purse."

"That big, black ugly thing? I wanted to burn it."

"My purse might be old, but my makeup is fine."

"You'll be photographed. *With my boss.* It's my job to make you look perfect for tonight. You will not be wearing over-the-counter." She shooed her into the bedroom. "Get that nap. Your body's about ten hours ahead of ours. You're probably exhausted. I won't have you looking tired in photos."

Feeling like a wayward child, Kristen walked into the bedroom, hating to admit that bossy, opinionated Stella was right. She was tired. But she was also happy. Going on one date was a small price to pay to get the computers she'd need. Aasera would have been so proud.

Plus, it wasn't like she'd accepted a date with Dean Suminski for real. She didn't have to fawn all over him or make goo-goo eyes. She also wouldn't have to laugh at his jokes, since he didn't make them. He was as serious as a person could be. Probably because he was a genius.

That thought caused her face to scrunch. She had no idea what a girl going out with a certifiable genius was supposed to do. But she could be polite…actually, she could be friendly. Which was probably what Dean Suminski really needed—a buffer. Someone outgoing enough that his seriousness wouldn't be so off-putting.

She could handle that.

As she slid under the covers, she remembered that Dean's friend Jason had said something about her job being to make him look normal. So that's what she should focus on doing. Behaving normally, so he would too.

She would do her best, even if he had declined her offer for him to visit Grennady and consider it as a place to relocate. He wasn't planning to move his company, he'd said. So she'd had no choice but to accept that. But at least she'd tried. And he'd really listened.

She had to give him points for that.

She woke hours later when bossy Stella walked into her room with her iPhone blaring Spanish music. "It's one of my Zumba tapes," she explained, proudly displaying her trim body. "I'm sure you have an exercise regimen to be so thin and fit."

"No," Kristen said, rolling out from under the covers. "Tossing hay keeps me fit."

"Tossing hay?"

"For the cows. Not just for them to eat, but for their beds. I live on a farm."

Stella's eyes widened. "No kidding. A real farm?"

"You have farms in the US."

"Yeah, I know. I've just never seen one. Or known anyone who lived on one," Stella said. She pointed to the bathroom. "Get your shower and be out in ten minutes. Hairdresser is already here. Makeup artist is on her way up."

Kristen walked into the bathroom and gasped. Everything was marble or glass. Eight showerheads peeked out at her. Fluffy white towels were arranged in baskets like bouquets. The soap smelled like heaven.

Too bad she only had ten minutes to enjoy it all. She couldn't even try the jets. Too much temptation to linger. She simply washed in the sweet-smelling soap and cleaned her hair with shampoo the scent of oranges.

After wrapping her wet head in a towel, she slid into the fluffy white robe on the back of the bathroom door. She stepped out into the sitting room of her suite to find at least ten people all talking at the same time.

When they saw her, everybody shut up for about three seconds, then started talking again.

"Who told her to wash her hair?"

"I like her eyes. I think we can go bold with them."

"I want to see the dress before I even think about makeup."

"We should do an updo."

"Does she have jewelry we should consider?"

Like an orchestra conductor, Stella raised her hands, then made a chopping motion. "Everybody shut up." She turned to Kristen. "You… in the chair."

Kristen walked over to the salon chair that had materialized in her sitting room while she'd been sleeping, sat down and turned herself over to the professionals.

Almost two hours later, Stella helped her slip into the black gown. She fastened her sparkly white gold necklace, then gave her the earrings. When they were in place, she handed Kristen a box.

"This is a gift. From Dean. He doesn't like to make a big deal out of these things, but he appreciates your help tonight."

As she took the box, a weird feeling enveloped her. It was one thing to keep the gown she'd need to help pull off his charade. Quite another to take a gift.

"I can't accept this."

Stella sighed. "You have to. He wants you to wear it tonight." She held up her hand. "Wait." Racing to a table by the door, she picked up another box. "These first."

She opened the box to find long black dinner gloves. "Gloves?"

"It's white tie," Stella explained, helping Kristen pull on the elbow-length gloves. "Way more formal than black tie. When I realized we'd forgotten them, I called the boutique and had these delivered. Open the gift."

Silky black gloves fumbling with the lid, she opened the second box and gasped. Her gaze jumped to Stella. "I don't care if he wants me to wear this, I can't accept it."

Without missing a beat, Stella took the diamond bracelet out of the box and slid it over Kristen's left hand and onto the glove. Sparkling against the black silk, the bracelet nearly blinded Kristen.

Stella laughed. "See why he bought this for you? When he saw the dress and gloves this afternoon—"

"He was here?"

"He was busy calling brokers, but I texted pictures." She shook her head. "He approves everything. Every detail. Anyway, when he saw the gloves and realized all your other jewelry was just white gold, he insisted on the diamonds."

"I can't keep them."

Stella laughed. "It isn't a request. Or an option. The bracelet is a necessary part of your outfit that becomes a thank-you gift. It's not my place to change that. If you don't want the bracelet, fight it out with Dean."

"I will."

Dean arrived in her hotel room at eight and Stella stepped back as if she were presenting Kristen as a completed project, not a person.

He took in the fancy upswept hairdo the stylist had given her, and then his gaze skimmed from the top of her dress to the tips of her toes. If another man had looked at her like that, she probably would have shivered, but his gaze was cool, efficient.

"She's perfect."

Stella beamed. "Of course she is." She grabbed her coat and purse. She said, "You two kids have fun," and then she left the hotel room.

Kristen sucked in a breath. "So I'm okay?"

"I already said you were perfect," he said, his voice businesslike and efficient. "Let's go."

Uneasiness wove through her. From his extremely chilly behavior, she had the odd sense that she'd done something wrong. But she hadn't. She'd agreed with everything he'd asked, including a stay in New York City that she hadn't planned on, a shopping trip and a Christmas party.

How could he be upset with her?

She picked up the black satin wrap that matched her gown and walked to the door with him. They rode down in the main elevator of the exclusive hotel in complete silence.

In the lobby, employees nodded and said, "Good evening, Mr. Suminski. Ms. Anderson," but other guests ignored them. They stepped outside into the cold December air and, glancing at her skimpy wrap, Dean rushed her into the limo.

She slid onto the seat. He slid on beside her. The limo pulled out into traffic.

The silence continued.

She peeked over at Dean who wore a black tux, white shirt, white vest and white bow tie. He looked clean and expensive and smelled divine. And for the first time it hit her that she was really on a date with him. One of the richest, most handsome men in the world.

The whole freaking world.

Her throat tightened. Her nerve endings buzzed. Right at that moment, sitting next to him, his money and social status took a backseat to his good looks. Never in a million years would a farm girl from Grennady ever date a guy like this. Not that the men in Grennady weren't handsome. But there was something about Dean Suminski that made her tingle. He was so pulled together and so smart, and those penetrating dark eyes of his were like onyx.

Of course he was also distant with her. Maybe not angry, but not exactly a guy who looked like he was on a date with a woman he liked. And it was her job to fool the world into thinking they were a couple. A happy couple.

She cleared her throat and said the first thing that came to mind. "So it really is white tie?"

He faced the window, clearly unhappy that he'd have to speak. "It's funny what rich people will think up to distinguish themselves."

"You're one of those rich people." She held up her arm, displaying the bracelet. Since he was angry anyway, they might as well settle this now. "By the way, I can't keep this."

He turned to her with a frown. "The bracelet?"

"Yes."

"Why not?"

"Because it's not right."

"You're helping me."

"We have a deal. Ten minutes after we shook hands, I signed the written agreement for *computers* in exchange for this date. No bracelet."

"The miracle of technology. I call my lawyer. He writes a simple, no-nonsense agreement, emails it to me and I print it. Everything goes at the speed of light these days."

She almost laughed at the way he tried to fool her. "Don't change the subject. As it is, we're equals. You start giving me bracelets and everything changes."

He tilted his head. "How so?"

"It makes our relationship personal. Plus, it's expensive. I don't need it—or want it."

When he only stared at her, she sighed. "Our deal should be professional. Things get messy when you mix personal things into business. I don't like messy."

He studied her face for a few seconds before he said, "It sounds like you've had a little experience in this."

She said nothing.

"If you want me to understand your point of view, you have to explain."

"I had a boyfriend who used me to get to the princess."

He studied her face again. "Taught you a lesson, huh?"

"And not a fun one." Actually, the idiot had broken her heart into a million pieces, made her feel like a fool and caused her to decide love wasn't for her. She would put her whole heart and soul into making Aasera's dream a reality because that had purpose and meaning. Love? She wasn't sure it existed, except for a few lucky people like Princess Eva.

"He used me to get to my boss, and when I figured it out, he said he wanted to marry me." She shook her head. Though it had been years, it still hurt. "It was ridiculous how simple he thought I was. It taught me never, ever mix business with pleasure."

He said, "Humph. I learned that lesson the hard way too."

"You did?"

"It's why Prince Alex hates me and why I also have a very strict policy about not mixing business with pleasure."

"That should make tonight easier. I don't want anything from you beyond what we've already agreed to." She laughed lightly. "Except maybe a good time. I haven't been out in forever."

He nodded. The stern expression on his face softened. She swore he almost smiled.

"At the end of the evening, I'll take back the bracelet."

She said, "Good," but she got a weird feeling, as if there was some kind of subtext to everything he said, and she didn't have the code for it.

The inside of the car grew silent again. She wondered what had happened to him that he'd learned the lesson, especially since it involved Prince Alex. Had the prince approached him for a favor? Or used him? She couldn't picture Prince Alex using anybody. Ever. It didn't make sense.

She waited a minute, hoping Dean would resume the conversation and explain, but of course he didn't. Curiosity wouldn't let her brain rest. And the limo was so quiet. Too quiet.

"So what happened?"

He peered over at her. "Excuse me?"

"What happened? Who used you?"

"I don't talk about my private life."

"You might not, but knowing why Prince Alex dislikes you would really help me when I have to explain to the princess that I approached you."

His gaze swung to hers. She didn't know if it was surprise or annoyance she heard in his voice when he said, "Princess Eva didn't send you?"

She shook her head. "It just didn't seem right that you weren't on the list of companies to try to woo to our country. Grennady is desperate to bring jobs for young people. And here you were with this great company and nobody was showing you what we had to offer. I was trying to do something good. I didn't know Prince Alex doesn't like you. When Princess Eva finds out I approached you, I'm screwed."

"Maybe you shouldn't tell her."

She shook her head. "Not telling her would be a lie of omission. I can't be dishonest."

His eyes narrowed as he studied her face. "Which means you knew you'd be telling them eventually. So you probably had an explanation in mind. Why not use that?"

She shrugged. "My endgame was to be able to tell them you'd be visiting in January to consider our country as the new home for your company. And they'd be so happy that they'd be glad I took the risk."

"I'm not coming to your country."

"Well, I know that now. And I know that has something to do with your feud with Prince Alex—"

"It's not a feud. He doesn't like me."

"Well, that's just shocking, considering your sparkling personality and all."

He laughed. "As if Alex Sancho is better."

"He adores my princess. He works as hard as any employee in the palace. He's kind to the staff. So, yeah. He's a good guy."

Dean sniffed. "He might be the happiest prince in the world now, but he wasn't always a good guy."

"I know that at one time he was sort of a playboy, gambler. I'm guessing the same is true with you. That you weren't always this dry and stuffy. I'm guessing that whatever happened between you and Alex, it happened when you were young—" she sneaked a peek at him "—and foolish."

He grimaced. "I was foolish, all right."

She groaned. "Tell me, so I know how to apologize to the princess and her husband for overstepping."

"Just say you're sorry."

"Please."

"No."

CHAPTER FOUR

THE NOTE OF finality in Dean's voice told Kristen the conversation was over. To seal the deal, his phone rang.

Miffed that he always got his way, she turned her gaze to the window. New York City was a sort of blur as the limo sped down the street, then they stopped at a traffic light. Not only could she see the lights and tinsel, ornaments and pine branches that decorated streetlamps and buildings, but the city itself was huge and modern.

She'd noticed that on her shopping trip that afternoon, but New York City was such a far cry from Grennady that it once again stole her breath. The crazy feeling that she was in over her head tried to sneak in and ruin her confidence, but she wouldn't let it. She might not be experienced, but she was educated.

And she had a goal to make Aasera's wish a reality. She would have to be tough enough that one city or one guy's opinion wouldn't shake her. She also had to be able to face the princess and her husband on her own, to apologize to Alex for doing something he hadn't wanted done.

She straightened her shoulders, sat taller in the limo seat. She could not—*would not*—fail because she let her confidence waver. She could do this.

When Dean finally hung up the phone, she didn't care what had happened between him and Prince Alex. Taking responsibility for this trip and responsibility for contacting the one person Alex hadn't wanted to be contacted was another step in her growth as a businessperson. Dean would probably call that lesson three, clean up your own messes.

Rather than endure the oppressive silence or let him think she was brooding because he wouldn't tell her why Alex hated him, she said, "The city's already decorated for Christmas."

"Yes. We seem to start earlier every year." He

paused then said, "Have you never been to New York before?"

She turned from the window to face him. His serious dark eyes caught hers. The now familiar tingle skipped along her skin as they studied each other.

He was so gorgeous that it was hard to believe no woman had snapped him up. Of course his personality did leave a lot to be desired. He might be so handsome that she sometimes lost her breath when their eyes met. But he was a grouch. Her job tonight was to make him seem normal—maybe even likable. She had to remember that task and do it, not lose her breath or wish he was different.

"I haven't been very many places. Except for university, I've been a homebody."

"Yet you want to start a charity that would technically be global."

His tone wasn't demeaning, more like curious, so she answered honestly. "This thing that I did with you," she said, pointing from herself to him and then back again. "It was like the first step in getting myself out of my shell and into the real world."

"Ambitious."

She laughed, glad he was no longer grouchy, just his usual stiff and formal. "Most people wouldn't think a flight to Paris would turn into a trip to New York. You're giving me a crash course in how rich people operate."

"Glad I can be of service. I want to do as much for you as you're doing for me. The more professional we keep this and the more equitable our deal, the easier it will be to manage."

"Lesson number four?"

"No, that relates back to lesson two. Don't mix business and pleasure."

"Right."

He frowned. "What was lesson three?"

"Clean up your own messes. I figured it out myself. Your disagreement with Alex has no bearing on the fact that I went behind the backs of the royal family to meet with you. So I have to own up to it and apologize."

"Good point." He peered over at her. "So we're officially counting them now?"

"The lessons?"

He nodded.

She laughed. "Sure. Why not?"

"You do recognize that this evening is four or five hours of me introducing you to important people. Potential contacts. You'd do well to make a good first impression and remember names."

"I never have a problem making a good first impression."

He smiled a real smile. "I have no doubt about that."

Fissions of pleasure skipped up her spine. If he continued being nice like this, the physical thing she felt for him might morph into a total attraction. Especially since the way he kept gazing into her eyes told her he was attracted to her too.

The limo stopped. The driver opened the door for them. Dean got out, and reached in to assist Kristen. The warmth of his fingers closing around hers caused her chest to freeze. Tingles rained down on her like snowflakes.

He gave a soft tug that brought her out of the limo and almost into his arms. Their eyes met and held. They might not want to mix business with pleasure, but the electricity humming through her made her wonder what it would be like to be on a date with him for real.

Crazy. Weird. Odd.

Those things popped into her head first. He might be good-looking, but he was also a genius who spoke his mind, always thought he was right and always wanted his own way. Those traits didn't make a good boyfriend—or date.

She pulled back, as he pulled back. Almost as if they'd both taken those two seconds to ask the question, *What if they acted on their attraction?* and both decided against it.

Dean put his hand on her elbow and turned her toward the hotel. They walked into the stately lobby and were directed to the elevator that would take them to the ballroom several floors up. When the doors closed, he immediately took his hand off her elbow and stuffed it in his pocket.

Those few seconds after he'd helped her out of the limo, when they'd stood face-to-face, a mere fraction of an inch apart, his whole body had tensed with wanting her, and he'd suddenly seen that his gut wasn't telling him she was somehow important. It was telling him he was a lot more attracted to her than he'd thought. Not because her eyes were pretty or because she had a long sloping back that led to the most perfect butt he'd ever seen. He *liked* her. *Her.*

She'd had hutzpah enough to question him about the situation with Alex. She'd easily confessed her fear about how she would explain approaching him to her boss. Then she'd admitted it was her own mess, and she'd clean it up.

He couldn't remember the last time anybody was so honest with him. So open. And the fact that he liked it confused him. He was a need-to-know person, who lived in a need-to-know world. Yet hearing about her, her background, her situation, pleased him.

Even so, starting something with her was wrong. He did not do relationships. Especially not with innocent women. So he stopped the pleasant hum buzzing through him.

The elevator door opened and her gasp of joy took his gaze to her face. Her green eyes sparkled. Her lush lips lifted into a glorious smile.

"It's so pretty."

To him the decorations were fairly standard. Evergreen branches outlined the arch doorway that led to the ballroom where white poinsettias in short fat fishbowls sat as centerpieces on round tables covered with red linen tablecloths. Crystal glasses sparkled in candlelight. White lights twinkled overhead like stars.

Putting his hand at the small of her back, Dean nudged her out of the elevator. "It's about normal." He frowned. "Your princess must take you nowhere."

"I'm a background person. But I'm changing that. And I appreciate this opportunity to step out of my comfort zone."

There was that honesty again. So pure and so simple, it almost made him relax. But that was absurd. Not only was getting involved with this woman out of his life plan, but also his company was in trouble. Instead of constantly being drawn into wondering about unwanted feelings, he needed to use this time to assure people that he wasn't out of touch. He was in control.

"Dean!"

Dean and Kristen turned toward the sound of the booming voice owned by George Perkins, the party's host. A tall, striking man, with snow-white hair and probing blue eyes, he held out his hand to Dean. "So glad you could come."

Dean said, "The pleasure is mine, George. Thank you for inviting me." He smiled at George's wife, who stood beside him. Petite and pretty, Lorraine glowed with happiness.

"Good evening, Lorraine." Then he turned to Kristen. "Kristen, these are George and Lorraine Perkins, our hosts for the evening." He faced their hosts and said, "This is my guest, Kristen Anderson."

Kristen shook hands with George and Lorraine. "The decorations are wonderful."

Lorraine brightened even more. Toying with the extravagant diamond necklace at her throat, she said, "Thank you. It's always a debate. Simple and elegant or over-the-top. This year I went with simple and elegant."

Kristen said, "Everything looks perfect."

A middle-aged couple walked up behind them and Dean took Kristen's elbow. "We'll see you inside," he said to George and Lorraine, as he guided Kristen into the ballroom.

"You should have told Lorraine you liked her necklace."

Dean stopped. "What?"

"Lorraine kept playing with her necklace. She clearly loves it. Noticing it would have pleased her."

Dean laughed. "Really? You want a guy to notice a necklace?"

"It couldn't hurt. Women love compliments. Plus, George probably bought it for her. Noticing would have made him happy too."

"Are you trying to tell me how to behave?"

"Sort of."

"Well, stop. I know what works for me in social situations and what doesn't."

"I think Jason disagrees with you."

He grabbed two flutes of champagne from a passing waiter. "Jason worries like an old woman."

"Maybe. But you must have agreed on some level or another or I wouldn't be here."

"You're here for appearances."

"Right. You want me to look normal, so you'll look normal." She tapped her index finger on her chin. "Hmm. That actually makes my case, doesn't it?"

He sighed. Though her logic was a bit twisted, she was correct. Jason wanted him to appear happy and she was happy. "Just don't say or do anything I'll regret."

"Fine. But if I'm supposed to be myself, I'm being myself."

She accepted the champagne from him and gazed around. Dean took the time she was preoccupied to study her dress, her fancy upswept hair. He almost told her she looked really pretty, but swallowed back the words. He already knew his attraction to her was stronger than he'd thought. Not complimenting her was part of his "don't tempt fate" policy.

He wondered what she'd think if he taught her that rule—don't tempt fate—and burst out laughing.

She pivoted to face him. "What?"

"I just thought of something when I looked at you."

Her face fell in dismay. "I look funny?"

He sobered. "No." The words *you're beautiful* almost popped out of his mouth, but he caught them again. "I told you, you're perfect. Stella did a perfect job." He quickly scanned the tables and said, "This way. My invitation says we're at table thirty-one."

As they searched for their table, they said hello to various couples and exchanged pleasantries. Dean introduced Kristen to everyone, but he didn't really pause long enough to talk with anyone, finally understanding Jason's strategy. He'd already called all the brokerage houses. He didn't need to say any more. What he needed to do was look calm and confident, happy to be out with a pretty girl.

When they paused to say hello to Mr. and Mrs. Norman Jenkins, Kristen said, "Mrs. Jenkins, your necklace is beautiful. Is it an heirloom?"

The tall, thin woman beamed. "Why, yes. It belonged to my grandmother."

"It's stunning." Kristen turned to Dean. "Isn't it?"

He stole a peek at her. It might be weird for him

to compliment a necklace, but Kristen pulled it off easily and had also put him in a position where he could simply agree and probably look like a nice guy.

"Yes. It's beautiful."

Mrs. Jenkins caught Kristen's hand. "It's so kind of you to notice. These days everyone seems to be captivated by new and shiny." She pressed her hand over the brooch-like necklace, which— surrounded by untold carats of diamonds—spar-kled like a bonfire. "I prefer old and familiar."

Norman Jenkins chuckled. "Which is why she's still married to me."

Kristen laughed. Dean smiled. Having Kristen with him really did ease him more naturally into conversations, especially since he'd realized he shouldn't talk about business.

The Jenkinses walked away happy, and Dean let Kristen take the lead in all their chats, and allowed her to compliment to her heart's delight. He drank his champagne and took another glass for himself and Kristen. He even found himself laughing once or twice.

Right before dinner, the Kauffmans sidled up

to them. A bubbly young couple who owned a PR firm that Suminski Stuff had used a time or two, and who had just had their first child, Pete and Belinda were more his age than most of the attendees.

After Dean introduced Kristen, she said, "We'd love to see a picture of your son. Wouldn't we, Dean?"

Trusting her, he said, "Sure."

The Kauffmans whipped out their phones. Belinda was the first to get her pictures up for viewing, and she handed her phone to Dean. On the screen was the oddest face he had ever seen. Bald head, bugging eyes, spit bubbles in the corners of the little boy's lips.

He honestly wanted to say something nice but his tongue stuck to the roof of his mouth.

Kristen smoothly said, "Oh, he's adorable! Such big eyes!"

Following her lead, Dean said, "Yes, big eyes." But ten minutes later, when the new parents were finally out of earshot, he turned to Kristen. "You deserve some kind of an award for keeping a straight face while looking at that kid."

She laughed. "He was adorable."

"No. He wasn't."

"Sure he was. All babies are cute in their own way."

"If you say so."

"Oh, Dean, life isn't about symmetry or perfection. It's about what makes a person unique, and that little boy's eyes were spectacular."

He said, "I guess," but what she'd said made real sense. Not just because the baby with the big eyes and bald head did look happy, but because he'd met all kinds in his world. Superstitious programmers who had lucky T-shirts. Marketing people who wore the latest fashions, and accountants who were never out of their suits. It took all of them to make Suminski Stuff successful. In spite of her naïvety, Kristen Anderson was pretty smart.

Relaxing another notch, he motioned her in the direction of their table, but she didn't make a move to walk toward it. She peered at him. "You haven't spent a lot of time around kids, have you?"

"No. And I plan to keep it that way."

"Really? You don't want to have kids of your own someday?"

"I wouldn't know the first thing about being a father."

"I've heard it comes naturally."

He gestured again for her to walk. "Not when you didn't have one to be an example."

Her face filled with sympathy. Apology filled her green eyes. "I'm so sorry. I forgot your parents were killed."

"It's fine."

She shook her head. "No. It's not fine. I should have thought that through before I made such a careless comment."

"Don't worry about it. It's hard to remember every little detail of somebody's bio."

"But that's an important one."

"Not really. I'm over it."

She held his gaze, her sympathetic eyes sending an odd feeling through him, a knowing that if he'd talk about this with her she'd understand.

"You're not over it or you wouldn't be so sure you don't want to have kids."

He laughed to ease the pressure of the knot in

his chest, the one that nudged him to say something honest when he couldn't be honest. He'd never told anyone anything but the bare-bones facts of his childhood. And one woman with pretty eyes—no matter how much she seemed to be able to get him to relax—wouldn't change that.

He stuck with the rhetoric that had served him well for the ten years he'd guided Suminski Stuff. "Being over it has little to do with the decision not to have kids. I don't just lack parenting skills, I also have an unusual job. In the past twenty-four hours I've been in two countries, crossed an ocean. There's no place in my life for a wife, let alone kids."

She caught his gaze and gave him the most puzzling look for about ten seconds, and then she finally said, "You know, that just makes you all the more a challenge."

"A challenge?"

"Sure." Her smile broadened, a bubble of laughter escaped. "Every woman wants to be the one who tames the confirmed bachelor and turns him into a family man."

She said it in jest. Her laugh clearly indicated she was teasing. But he could picture them in the master bedroom of his Albany estate, white curtains billowing in the breeze from open French doors. White comforter on a king-size bed. Her leaning on pillows plumped against a tufted headboard. Holding a baby.

His baby.

He shook his head to clear it of the totally absurd thought.

She pointed to a discreet sign on a table only a few feet away. She said, "Thirty-one," and started moving toward it.

He breathed a sigh of relief. Not that the vision was gone, but also that she'd finally started walking. They reached their seats and he pulled out her chair for her.

She sat. "I want lots of kids."

He sat beside her. The discussion might not have changed, but it had shifted off him and to her. That he could handle. "While you're globe-trotting for your schools?"

"There are ways around that. Like nannies.

And my mom." She laughed. "I don't have a doubt that she'll be a hands-on grandmother."

His breath stalled as a memory of his own grandmother popped into his head. If she'd been "hands-on" it had been with her palm to his bottom when she'd decided that he'd misbehaved.

He rose and shook hands when another couple arrived at their table, working to bring himself back from the memory of his grandmother paddling him for spilling milk when he was five or asking for a baseball mitt when he was seven.

But as he frantically struggled to block his bleak, solitary childhood from his brain, Kristen said, "I can't imagine not having my own family. I mean, I love my parents and all, but I want a crack at being a mom. Teaching someone everything I know."

An empty feeling filled him and on its heels came an envy so strong it was a battle not to close his eyes. She must have had a wonderful childhood. But being jealous was stupid, pointless. He'd gotten over his hollow beginnings years ago. Being lonely had forced him to entertain himself, and that ultimately had made him rich. He was pragmatic about his past. So, it shouldn't make him feel bad that his childhood had been crap. Just as it shouldn't make him jealous that Kristen was so confident in her decision to have kids. Or make him wonder how much fun the family she intended to create would be.

Dinner was served, a very untraditional meal of steak and vegetables. To his surprise, Kristen ate with gusto. While the wives of his counterparts pushed their food around their plates, Kristen ate every bite of her steak and was on the edge of her seat waiting for dessert. Crème brûlée.

Then he realized they hadn't fed her all day. He'd had a sandwich and fries delivered to his office as he'd made all his calls to brokers, but he'd forgotten to tell Stella that Kristen hadn't eaten. And skinny Stella was known to skip meals.

He leaned over and whispered, "I'm sorry we forgot lunch."

Her head tilted as she smiled. "I slept the day away. I was fine."

Her pretty face made his breath stutter again. Her smooth, pink skin glowed in the candlelight.

Her genuine smile warmed him. She wasn't faking having a good time.

And hadn't she said she needed a good time?

Ignoring the odd happiness that filled him when he realized he'd done something to please her, he motioned to her plate. "You were obviously starving."

She frowned. "You think I was starving because I ate all my steak?" She burst out laughing. "I eat like that all the time."

Her laugh made him laugh. Muscles he hadn't even realized were knotted untangled. She really was the most honest, most open person he'd ever met. He might feel the need to fight all the crazy feelings she inspired, but he simply could not help relaxing around her.

Gina McMurray, wife of Tim McMurray, leaned across the table. "I didn't mean to eavesdrop but, oh, my God, I would love to eat like that."

Sherri Johnson said, "Me too. I can't, though. I'd blow up like a cow. What's your secret?"

Kristen said, "Good metabolism probably. But my parents own a dairy farm. I still do my fair share of the chores."

Sherri nodded. "When I ran around after my kids, I didn't have to worry about weight, either."

Gina said, "I guess it's all about moving."

As the women chatted, Dean glanced over at Kristen and let her work her magic. He now trusted her enough not to worry about what she'd say or how she'd say it. He liked hearing her tell their tablemates about her life. She was *interesting*. She worked for a princess, lived on a farm very different from anything he'd ever experienced and had a degree that she intended to use to start a charity that built schools. While she did all that, she wanted to have kids, and teach them to be citizens of the world.

It was no wonder he liked her.

She was amazing.

George Perkins walked on stage and took the microphone. He wished everybody a merry Christmas and announced the dancing would begin. All the men at his table asked their wives to dance and Dean knew it would look odd if he and Kristen didn't join them on the floor.

He rose and held out his hand. "Shall we?"

She smiled. "I'd love to."

He led her to the dance floor and took her into his arms, where she fit perfectly. She was the right height for him. She was pretty. She had just enough sophistication that it didn't impinge on her natural, innocent charm. She ate when she was hungry. She wanted to have kids. She wanted to change the world.

All his crazy feelings around her came into focus, and he nearly stopped dancing. She wasn't just amazing. She was the perfect woman for him. *Of course he was attracted to her. Of course he wanted her.*

If there was such a thing as the woman of his dreams, it was Kristen.

Happiness mixed with a knowing that expanded his chest with a fierce need to kiss her, and his heart with a longing to keep her—to never let her out of his sight—that he'd never felt before.

It also explained the unwanted vision of her with his child, the way he could relax with her and why he couldn't stop staring at her face.

Some crazy, romantic part of himself wanted a future with her.

But it was all for nothing.

Not only did he have a really crappy upbringing that meant he had no idea what a real family looked like, no idea how to be a husband or a father, but there was also the matter of why Alex Sancho hated him.

If that wasn't enough to make him all wrong for her, he had a one-track mind. His company. Even if she found him as attractive and interesting as he found her, she should run like the wind away from him.

Once she got to know him, she probably would.

He stepped back, sliding his hands down her arms until he could take her hands. "I'm suddenly very, very tired. Let's go back to the table."

Her eyes sought his as her lush mouth, her perfect, oh-so-kissable mouth twisted in confusion. "We aren't going to mingle?"

He once again used pragmatism to overcome her questions.

"I might mingle later. I'm not sure. Jason just wanted me to put in an appearance. I think we've done more than that."

Before she could say anything, Dean caught

her hand and began to maneuver through the crowd, toward their table, pulling her with him. Regret wobbled through him, but he wondered why. This was his life. And he was essentially happy with it. He was a rich man, doing work he loved. He wouldn't feel bad that he was attracted to a woman he couldn't have. He had many, many things to be grateful for.

They didn't quite get to their seats before Winslow and Julia Osmond, who owned one of the biggest brokerage houses in New York, ambled up to him.

"I see your stock is hanging tough."

"Thanks to you," Dean agreed. He'd had a good chat with Winslow that afternoon. Even though he'd created an informal "no talking about business" rule for this party, this was a chance to reinforce what he'd said.

Kristen tapped his arm. "I thought we agreed no shoptalk tonight."

The gesture was sweet, familiar, and longing whispered through Dean again. Longing for a life, a relationship, things he'd never wanted before. It was confusing. Frustrating. Ridiculous.

Winslow Osmond said, "I got the same lecture." He smiled at Kristen. "Where did you two meet?"

"Paris."

Julia Osmond said, "Oh, how romantic."

Kristen laughed. "Somewhat romantic. We actually find ourselves on opposite ends of a business thing. I work for Princess Eva Latvia of Grennady."

Julia caught her arm. "Oh, darling! Didn't she just marry that gorgeous prince from Xaviera?"

"Yes. Alexandros Sancho. They're in Xaviera right now at the end of a vacation celebrating American Thanksgiving. Alex's brother Dom is married to an American and his dad married Princess Ginny's mom, Rose."

Winslow laughed. "Now, that's going to be a complicated family tree." He faced Dean. "What business does your company have with Grennady?"

Dean's gaze slowly meandered to Kristen, then back to Winslow. When in doubt, go with the truth. If he and Kristen were alone, that would be lesson five.

"Kristen would like me to consider relocating my company there. Unfortunately, I'm not in a position to even consider it."

"Why not?"

Dean sort of laughed. "We are in a bit of a hurry to get that series of games ironed out. As I told you in our phone call today, I *will* be beta testing the new version by mid-January. I'm not going to disrupt people who are already stalled."

Winslow glanced at his glass of whiskey, then back at Dean. "You've never considered that a change of scenery might do them good?"

When Dean frowned, Winslow said, "Maybe their creativity would return if you sent them to a country that's known for fresh air and fresh snow. Somewhere they can get outside and do something physical that will revitalize them. Grennady sounds like the perfect choice to me."

"Where are your offices?" Julia asked.

"Manhattan," Winslow answered for Dean. "His employees fight to get into the city, then they're in a high pressure situation trying to fix or finish a product that's obviously in trouble, then they fight to get back home." He caught Dean's gaze. "No rest for these guys and gals."

Dean recognized a criticism when he got one, but he smiled at Winslow. "That's certainly an interesting observation."

"That's not an observation. It's a fact." Winslow clasped Dean's shoulder. "You know what? A few of my associates and I are having lunch tomorrow. It's our little Christmas celebration. I'd love to have you and Kristen join us."

"Oh, well…" Dean fumbled for an excuse, but his mind went blank. He couldn't ask Kristen to stay another day, could he?

"Oh, come on. You want to miss the chance to talk to CEOs for some of the biggest companies in the city?" Winslow winked at Kristen. "If nothing else, you should want to show Kristen off."

Kristen laughed. "It sounds fun."

Considering Kristen's response approval of a sort and not wanting to miss the opportunity, Dean said, "Have your staff send me the restaurant name and time."

Osmond slapped him on the back. "You bet."

As he and his wife walked away, Dean turned to Kristen. "If you only answered that way to be polite, I can show up alone. It's not a big deal."

But Kristen glanced behind her, watching Winslow and his wife mingle into the crowd. "He's pretty influential?"

"He is the definition of *influential*. If you look in the dictionary, his picture would be beside the word *influential*."

"Then we should go."

"Seriously? You don't mind staying in New York another day?"

She laughed lightly. "Tomorrow's Saturday. It's fine." She frowned. "Except." She looked up and into his eyes again. "Will I be able to wear the black pants and white blouse I flew over in?"

Regret surged through him that he'd put her in an uncomfortable position. Luckily, he could fix it. "We'll get you new clothes."

"Stella?"

"No, this time I'll take you. We'll have breakfast, then go back to the boutique where you got this gown."

"Okay."

She was such a good sport that he almost felt guilty taking advantage of her. Except he needed her. And she *was* a good sport. "I swear tomorrow at three you'll be on your way to the airport, and in the air headed for Grennady by five."

But the assurance that he'd get her home the next day didn't stop the nagging feeling in the pit of his stomach.

Their deal wasn't balanced now, and he hated owing someone.

CHAPTER FIVE

THE NEXT MORNING, Kristen woke, showered and dressed in her simple white blouse and black pants. She'd carefully hung them the day before so they weren't wrinkled, but this was day two of wearing the same clothes, and she had to wear these home. She might have to rinse out her blouse when she returned.

As she stepped into the sitting room of her suite, her hotel phone rang.

Confused, she picked it up and cautiously said, "Hello?"

"It's Dean. I'm in the hotel dining room. I've ordered coffee. Come down when you're ready."

The sound of his voice made her heart light, but she squelched the silly feeling that had started the night before by reminding herself that she'd fallen desperately in love with Brad, a man who had also used her. She'd ended up hurt and disillusioned. Just because Dean was coming right out and telling her he was using her, it only made him marginally better than Brad. Or maybe not better. More like honest. Especially since the way he'd pulled away from her on the dance floor had all but proven she was safe with him. A man who didn't want to touch her didn't want to get involved with her.

And she shouldn't want to get involved with anybody, either. Especially not such a difficult man. She was about to embark on the journey of a lifetime. Beginning an international charity, something with the potential to change the world, would be all-consuming. She didn't have time for a romance until her schools were off the ground.

She took the elevator to the lobby, found the restaurant and walked to the table where Dean sat. He rose and her stomach fell to the floor.

Wearing jeans and a comfortable olive green sweater, he barely resembled the angry man she'd met the morning before in Paris. He looked young, approachable. And if the smile on his face was any indicator, he was very happy to see her.

The joyful feeling bubbled up in her again, the sense that there was nowhere she'd rather be than with him. Because it was true. He was so handsome in that sweater and jeans. And he looked happy…

How was she supposed to resist that?

He pulled out her chair. "I hope you slept well."

"Since I'd napped all yesterday afternoon, I was glad to have had a few glasses of champagne to make me drowsy."

A waiter walked over and poured Kristen a cup of coffee from the carafe already on the table.

Dean said, "I'll have the bacon and eggs breakfast." He faced her with another smile. "Kristen?"

She could barely say, "I'll have the same." Her heart did a crazy dance in her chest every time he smiled at her. She tried reminding herself of Brad, but it didn't help. With Dean's face a study in happiness and her attraction to him tapping on her shoulder, the giddy feeling rolling through her wouldn't let anything negative in.

As the waiter walked away, happy Dean faced her again. "I realized last night that your attending another event with me warrants another agreement." He pulled a document from beside his plate. "This is a second agreement that takes the place of the one we signed yesterday. Instead of a hundred thousand dollars' worth of computers, it's now two hundred thousand."

Her eyes bulged. "Two hundred thousand dollars' worth of computers?"

As she took the agreement from his hands, she realized *this* was why he was so happy. He wasn't smiling because of her. He wasn't happy to see her. He was happy that their deal wasn't lopsided. By giving her more computers, he was no longer accepting a favor. They were even.

All the crazy feelings rumbling around inside her stopped instantly.

She glanced up at him. "You don't like owing people, do you?"

His head tilted. "Because I'm continuing our arrangement?"

"Because you won't let me do you a favor."

He shrugged. "This relates more to the 'don't mix business with pleasure' rule."

"Nope. I think we've entered new rule territory. You don't like anyone doing anything for you."

He fiddled with his linen napkin. "Good business people keep things balanced. The revised agreement is simply a way to do that."

"Sure it is." She paused for a moment as the waiter brought their bacon and eggs, then said, "And what about the clothes you're buying me?" She caught his gaze. "And the bracelet you didn't take back last night. If you want everything even and balanced, then I'm going to have to pay you for the clothes. And God only knows what I'll owe you for the bracelet."

He shook his head. "The clothes and bracelet are the cost of doing business."

She scrunched her face. "What cost of doing business?"

"You are here at my request. You cannot wear the same clothes every day. Hence, it's my responsibility to clothe you."

"You are a piece of work."

He frowned. "Because I like to keep things balanced?"

"Whatever you call it. It's kind of weird. And don't think I'm not noticing that you always have to win arguments."

"I win because I'm right."

She picked up her fork and began eating, deciding she wasn't even going to try to debate that. But after the first delectable bite of toast, for some odd reason or another she pictured him as a child, a genius in an elementary school filled with ordinary kids, and she laughed.

"I'll bet that attitude worked out really well on the playground."

He shook his head. "It didn't. That's how I met Jason. When things would turn ugly, he would race over and run interference before somebody decked me or before I hit someone. He was also smart enough to direct me to a few YouTube videos that taught me how to fight." He smiled again. "I got pretty good."

And how was she supposed to not laugh at that? "How long were you in public school?"

He chewed a bite of toast, obviously pondering that. "Every year until somebody finally figured out I might be a genius. At thirteen, I took a test that proved it and instantly got offers for scholarships for university. I spent one year at MIT and in the end decided that wasn't for me."

He'd *discarded* the Massachusetts Institute of Technology? "Seriously?"

"The thing was, I already knew everything I needed to know about computers. As a kid, I'd bought a few books, torn apart a few motherboards and I was up to speed. But I didn't know anything about business." He shrugged. "So that's what I studied. I knew I wanted to work in this field, but not as a grunt. I wanted to own the company. So I needed to study how to run one."

And he'd figured all this out at fourteen. "Smart."

He laughed. "Exactly."

She let that settle in for a second, her mind wrapping around the double meaning and not able to let it go. "Did you just make a joke?"

"I guess I did."

And he seemed genuinely surprised. Which was equal parts of cute and breath-stealing. She'd seen him relaxing with her the night before. She'd noticed him staring at her as if he couldn't look away. He was every bit as attracted to her as she was to him. And he wasn't after money, or an introduction to the princess. If anything, he *didn't* want to meet her royal family. He needed her to pretend to be his girlfriend and if anything he was more than honest about it.

It was getting harder and harder to see him as someone like Brad. And harder and harder not to see how he relaxed around her, how he talked to her, how they clicked.

They finished their breakfast and walked outside into the sunny December morning, where his limo awaited. In a few minutes, they were back at the boutique, where Jennifer, the store manager from the day before, happily greeted them. Kristen hadn't seen the price of her gown yesterday afternoon, but she guessed that if Jennifer got a commission, it had been a hefty one.

"Good morning!"

Dean said, "Good morning. We're going to an

important lunch in a few hours, but our trip was so unexpected that Kristen didn't have time to pack. So we'd like to see everything she'll require for an upscale lunch."

Jennifer all but bowed. "Of course."

Dean shoved his hands in the pockets of his black leather jacket. "I was thinking in terms of something like a suit."

Kristen balked. "A suit? What am I? Seventy?"

"A suit is appropriate," Dean said, glancing around at the various styles of clothes they offered.

"A sweater dress can be just as appropriate."

"It's a business lunch," Dean argued.

"Not really. It's a Christmas lunch with friends or a bunch of guys you hope to make your friends," Kristen countered, deciding this was one argument he was not winning. "And besides, I'm not a part of your business." She almost said, "I'm supposed to be your girlfriend," but she caught the way Jennifer was looking at them, her wide eyes speaking of her curiosity. So, she smiled and said, "I'm your girlfriend."

Dean's expression shifted from determined to confused.

But Jennifer seemed to love that tidbit. "This explains so much about yesterday," she said enthusiastically. She faced Dean. "From the things she chose while she was with Stella, I know that you can trust her taste." She turned to Kristen. "And I agree with you. The right sweater dress will be more than appropriate."

She motioned to the dressing room. "Give me two seconds to pull my three favorites."

Dean scowled.

But as Jennifer walked away, Kristen laughed. "Who would you rather do business with? Someone who cowers or someone who knows what she's doing?"

He sighed and brushed his hand in the direction of the curtained-off changing area. "Just go get ready to try on the dresses."

She slipped into the mirrored room and removed her pants and shirt. Jennifer stepped in holding three sweater dresses.

"The red," she said, hanging it on the first hook, "Because I think you'll look beautiful in it. Blue because it's a little more sedate for Grumpy Pants out there. And black because I know his type. He'll pick the black because he doesn't want anyone looking at you."

Kristen's face flushed with color. "He's really not possessive."

"Oh, honey, they're all possessive. But if you don't believe me. Start with the red, give him the heart attack he wants to have, move on to the blue and go to the black. He'll pick the black."

Doing as she had been told, Kristen slipped into the red dress. The soft knit clung to her curves, but not obnoxiously. It just looked like a pretty dress.

When she stepped out of the dressing room, Dean's back was to her. She said, "Here's dress one," and he turned around.

Seeing Kristen in the red dress, Dean swore his heart exploded. It nicely cruised her curves but not indecently. It was a pretty dress that complimented a gorgeous figure. And it came to her knees. There was nothing to be upset about.

But blonde, green-eyed Kristen was certainly

heart-stopping in the striking red dress. Then he realized it wasn't the dress. It was Kristen. In anything other than black pants and a white shirt, she was going to be a knockout.

He tried to say something, but his tongue was stuck to the roof of his mouth.

Jennifer laughed. "Let's try the blue one."

She shooed Kristen into the curtained off room and in a few minutes Kristen returned in the blue knit dress.

"Wow." Okay. He'd tried to stop that but couldn't. The blue dress somehow highlighted the pale green color of her eyes and made her look spectacular. "That's..." He cleared his throat. "Very pretty."

Jennifer smiled. "Okay. On to dress three."

This time, Kristen emerged in a black dress. It looked simple and elegant. Yes, it still accented the same perfect figure, but not quite so enthusiastically.

"I like this one."

Jennifer laughed, but Kristen said, "I like the red!" Her eyes narrowed. "And you liked the red too."

He sucked in a breath. He'd been struck speechless by the red. She'd have had to be blind not to see that. "I did."

"Then why are we picking the black one?"

"Because I don't want Winslow or his friends to have a stroke."

She sighed. "Okay. You know what? I'm going to buy the red one for myself." She picked up the tag from the sleeve, glanced at the price and her mouth fell open. "Or not. I don't think my parents paid this much for our last cow."

A laugh burst from Dean. "If you really want the red one, I'll buy the red one too. But I'm asking nicely for you to wear the black one to the lunch."

"I can't let you buy the red one," she mumbled, turning to walk into the dressing room again.

"Well, you're going to need something to fly home in. You can't wear those black pants and white shirt again."

The curtain flew closed in a resounding swish. She was mad.

She was mad?

Why?

He approached the closed curtains and called out, "I'm happy to buy the red dress."

"Just stop." The order came from behind the curtain. "I have plenty of clothes at home. I don't need the red dress and before you get to harping about what I'm wearing home, I am not going to let you pay God knows what for a pair of blue jeans."

Ignoring her, Dean motioned to Jennifer to get a pair of jeans, knowing she'd have Kristen's size from choosing the dresses that day and the gown the day before. Then he pointed at the sweaters.

When she returned, he whispered, "Add shoes or boots and socks…whatever else she's going to need to stay this extra day."

Jennifer disappeared into the racks as Kristen walked out. Her chin high, she headed toward the cash register. "I do not want the red dress."

He said, "Fine."

She stopped, faced him. "You're losing an argument?"

"No. I'm simply not arguing over something stupid. I was happy to buy you the dress as a thank-you."

"Wouldn't we have to draw up another agreement for that?"

He sighed. "I'm not that bad."

"No. But for a guy who talks about balance you certainly don't see my side of the story."

"And what side is that?"

"That I don't want to take gifts. I have some pride. And I have a job. I can afford to buy my own clothes. I just can't afford to buy them in this shop."

"Okay."

Her eyebrows rose. "You're losing another argument?"

He shook his head. "No. I'm doing what you told me to do. I'm seeing your side of things."

"Good."

"Good."

He directed her to walk to the checkout, where Jen stood beaming. He guessed she worked on commission.

She scanned the tag on the black knit dress and a black wool coat. "I noticed that your coat is hip length and to wear a dress you'll need a longer one." She smiled hopefully. "I picked the most useful, inexpensive coat we have."

Kristen nodded.

Jennifer scanned the tag of a pair of black stilettoes. She looked up at Kristen. "I remembered your shoe size from yesterday. The shoes you wore under the gown had such a small heel. I think you'll need these."

This time Kristen sighed.

Dean quietly said, "I don't know a lot about women's shoes but we've trusted Jennifer so far. If she says you need the shoes, you probably need the shoes."

Kristen rolled her eyes.

Jennifer shoved the shoes into a shopping bag, then picked up a pair of jeans and a bright red sweater.

"I hope those are for Stella."

He cleared his throat. "You know you need something to fly home in."

She eyed the red sweater.

Dean saw the flicker of longing that sparked in her eyes before she could bank it, and he said a word he didn't often say. "Please." What was the point of having money if he couldn't spend it to make someone happy?

She faced him. "It's not a gift? It's not you saying thank you to me? It's a necessity?"

He nodded. "Absolutely. Unless you want to wash out your blouse in the sink of your hotel room."

"I'd considered it."

"And it would dry wrinkled."

She drew in a breath. "Okay. I do feel a little slimy in these clothes."

"Good. I mean, not good that you're slimy. Because you don't look slimy. Good that you can get a shower and fly home refreshed."

Kristen rolled her eyes and looked away.

A strange relief poured through him, followed by something he almost didn't recognize. Pride. She'd really wanted that sweater and he'd bought it for her. It gave him the most amazingly wonderful feeling.

As Jennifer lifted the sweater and jeans off the counter and slid them into the bag, a black lace bra and panties revealed themselves.

The store clerk winced. "You did say to get everything she needed."

His heart kicked against his ribs. He could see tall, slender, nicely endowed Kristen in the black bra and panties…and the black stilettos. He tried to say, "Maybe another color would be better," but it came out, "Navy anubber color would 'e 'etter."

Kristen looked at him through her peripheral vision. "You don't like black?"

Good God, he loved the black. But he realized that he'd have to sit through an entire lunch with several influential people, knowing she had black lace panties and bra under that dress.

He tugged at the collar of his sweater, but said, "Get whatever color you want."

She faced Jennifer. "I'll keep the black."

He had his chauffeur drive them to her hotel and carried her bags up to her suite for her. She opened the door with her key card and let him enter first.

"Where do you want these?"

"The chair will do."

He set the bags on the chair and headed for the door. "I'll be back in about two hours."

She nodded and he left breathing a long sigh of relief. He would go to his penthouse, take a cold shower and return a calm man, who would not, absolutely would not, remember the sexy black lace panties and bra she'd have under that sedate dress.

CHAPTER SIX

DEAN WAS QUIET when he picked Kristen up at her hotel room at noon. The drive to the restaurant was also quiet, and Kristen was glad. It wasn't that she was angry about him buying her clothes. It was that he was so flippant about doing everything he wanted, but anything she did had to be part of an agreement.

When they walked into the restaurant, Dean didn't even say his name. The maître d' smiled and waved him forward, leading them to a private room in the back. Decorated for the holiday with evergreen branches bathed in white twinkle lights and a sophisticated poinsettia centerpiece on the large round table, the warm space welcomed them.

As Winslow had said, the group was small. Eight men in dark suits like Dean's. Eight women in everything from elegant skirts and jackets to slimming sheaths. In her black knit dress, Kristen fit in as if she belonged there.

But she didn't. She and Dean entered to a conversation about European vacations, and Kristen suddenly felt like a bumpkin. She was twenty-four, the executive assistant to a princess, who did have a degree, and who wanted to start a foundation that would build schools—but who knew no one. She'd been nowhere...

Well, except to Paris, where she'd picked up with this gorgeous, crazy, somewhat obsessive-compulsive guy, and was now pretending to be his date.

As Dean made introductions, she smiled and said, "It's a pleasure to meet you all," reminding herself that this was part of her new reality. She had to learn to schmooze prospective donors, speak intelligently about her cause and find support.

Dean pulled out her chair and she sat. He sat beside her.

Mrs. Arthur Flannigan, a woman who looked to be in her eighties, leaned across the table.

"Julia tells me you work for Princess Eva of Grennady."

"Yes, I'm her executive assistant."

"Sounds exciting."

Kristen laughed nervously. Everybody assumed that because she worked for a woman who would someday be a queen, she had a fantastic job and glamorous life. But it was Eva who traveled while Kristen stayed behind and kept up with emails.

"Some days my work is exciting. Other days, it's just like any other assistant's job."

Dean slid his arm across the back of her chair. "Kristen is about to leave her post to begin organizing a charity that will build schools in third world countries."

Mrs. Flannigan's eyes lit. "Really? That's quite an undertaking."

"Having worked for a princess," Dean said, "she's up on world politics. She knows what she's getting into."

Kristen sat a little taller. Not only did it feel right to have his arm around her, but also he seemed genuinely proud of her. She might not travel, but she did know world politics. Working for Eva had taught her a lot. Now she just had to figure out how to use it.

"I hear your company is in a spot of trouble," Mrs. Flannigan said, changing the subject as she smiled at Dean.

He shrewdly returned her smile. "Nothing I can't handle."

Winslow leaned toward Mrs. Flannigan. "Kristen and Dean met because she flew to Paris to get time with him to persuade him to relocate Suminski Stuff to Grennady."

Mrs. Flannigan's face brightened. "Really? Well, my dear, you are quite the adventurer."

All the pride she'd felt fled as her chest tightened. No matter how much she'd seen working for Eva, she wasn't really an adventurer. She was a shy woman with a big goal, who milked cows and baled hay. And being in this room, with a small group of influential people, she suddenly wondered about her sanity. How the hell did she ever think she could start a charity that would change the world?

Dean's arm slid from the back of her chair to

her shoulders. The reassuring feeling that she wasn't alone pumped air back into her lungs and restarted her breathing.

"She's not much of an adventurer, but she's got a heart of gold and I'm watching her grow more confident by the day. I have no doubt she can do this."

His belief in her revived her confidence. But she also realized this was the second time he'd spoken as if he knew her. Or at least knew things about her. The first time had been the day they'd met, on the plane, when he'd told Jason about her economics degree. He could have looked that up. He could have also guessed she was growing in confidence from the changes in the way she dealt with him since she'd first approached him in Paris. But her heart of gold? How would he know that?

They spent three hours with the business people and their spouses. It had surprised Kristen to learn Mrs. Flannigan, not Arthur, was the owner of the brokerage firm that didn't want to downgrade Dean's stock. They wanted him to get his prototype to another round of beta testers and roll it out, which was why Winslow had invited him to this lunch.

The group had ideas for how Dean could jump-start his staff's creativity. Winslow had even suggested that Dean should consider temporarily moving the team to Grennady, if only for the next six weeks or so, to get them away from the daily grind and hopefully motivate them. Especially since it would give him a chance to investigate a permanent move.

Kristen's ears had perked up at that, but Dean had blown off the idea. By the time they got back into the limo for the drive home, her head spun. First, she knew Winslow's idea was a good one. Why not send the Suminski Stuff team to Grennady to finish the project? Then she and Princess Eva would have tons of time to persuade him to move there permanently. Except Dean didn't like Prince Alex. Or, as Dean had said, Prince Alex didn't like him. Second, she hadn't forgotten the way he knew things about her and dropped facts at the oddest times. And while part of her itched to ask him about that, her mission for her country was more important.

"You should move your people to Grennady for the next six weeks. Let them celebrate Christmas on our snow-covered ski slopes and get refreshed enough that they can finish your project."

"It will take more than ski slopes to get my people moving. Winslow was being optimistic when he suggested that."

"Or maybe he's right."

"You just want me in your country for six weeks so you can give me a hard sell."

She should have realized he would see right through that and winced. "Would it be so bad?"

"I already told you Alex hates me."

"Why?"

He caught her gaze and smiled. "Must be my sparkling personality."

He'd made another joke? She struggled not to gape at him.

"You're a nice guy." Even as the words came out of her mouth she knew she meant them. He was a nice guy. A good guy. A very, very smart guy. But a guy who was deep down, very nice. "Something happened between you and Alex."

When he didn't answer, she sighed. "You have

a best friend that you've kept the whole way since middle school. You must have looked me up on the internet because you know things about me, and you remember them enough to get them into the right places in the conversation. That's not just smart, it's considerate. I'm thinking your reputation for being mean is highly exaggerated."

He peeked over at her again. "Or maybe you bring out the best in me."

In the silence of the limo, their gazes locked. Her heart stumbled in her chest. The warmth of connection flowed through her. Even as it filled her with wonder, it scared her to death. They were using each other. He was buying her things she didn't want. They were making friends under false pretenses. So why did they keep having these odd, intimate moments that felt honest?

Dean quietly said, "You did really well at that lunch. I sometimes see your confidence dip, but it shouldn't."

"And how would you know?"

"For starters, you have a natural poise. But I

also talked to a few people. Everyone says you're full of energy and dedication." He frowned. "Though I have to admit I am curious about the cause you chose."

She said nothing, a little tired of the way he knew so much more about her than she knew about him.

"You're not going to share?"

"I'll tell you that story, if you tell me a story about you."

"Okay. Go ahead."

"Oh, no. I know this scam. I'll tell you how I chose my charity and suddenly the limo will be at the hotel and you'll stay Mr. Mysterious."

He laughed. "Mr. Mysterious?"

She shrugged. "That's how you look to me. If it isn't in your bio, I don't know it."

"All right. I'll go first. What do you want to know?"

"I want to know what happened between you and Alex."

He winced. "Right for the jugular. You couldn't settle for hearing the story of how I was a poor kid, raised by a grandmother who was too tired for another child, who got under-wear for Christmas?"

She knew he'd meant to be funny, but once again she could hear the sadness in his voice and picture him as a little boy, alone, quiet. She was suddenly very grateful Jason had come into his life, and wished with all her heart that he had other people in his life, so many that he'd never be alone again.

"I can guess what you went through as a child." Her gaze crawled over to meet his. "But it's hard for me to understand how Prince Alex dislikes you when he loves everybody."

"I tried to steal his girlfriend."

Kristen couldn't help it. She laughed. "That's not enough to make him hate you."

"It's a much longer story." He took an exaggerated breath. "He had a girlfriend, Nina, who was the daughter of a Saudi prince I was schmoozing for funding when I first started out. Nina came into her dad's office one day when I was there. She smiled at me, and the prince thought this was a good opportunity to get his daughter away from Alex, who, at the time, was a gambler."

"Her dad wanted you to put a wedge between them?"

"Actually, her dad thought she and I were better suited for each other. And though he didn't say the words, he more or less tied his investing into my company to me hanging around Nina, trying to steer her away from Alex."

"That's awful."

"It isn't, when you remember that Alex wasn't a nice guy. He was the spoiled prince of a filthy rich country. He had access to more money than God and did what he wanted, including take Nina for granted and ignore her most days."

Though it was difficult to picture Alex that way, Kristen had to admit she'd heard those rumors.

"At first, I just started showing up at the places Nina frequented. Bars. The marina. A club or two. Then she accepted a date." He cleared his throat. "I fell head over heels in love with her, but she was only using me to make Alex jealous. And it worked. He stopped gambling, started paying attention to her and proposed."

Kristen's heart sank, as little pieces of things

began to fall together in her head. Not just about Dean being an inexperienced kid hanging around jet-setters, who now had a rule about not mixing business with pleasure, but also about Prince Alex. She remembered the princess telling her that Alex had had his heart broken when he was younger, when his fiancée had died.

The magnitude of the loss almost overwhelmed her and she whispered, "Nina died, didn't she?"

Dean quietly said, "In a boating accident after an argument with me. For a while Xaviera's royal guard investigated me, but I was nowhere near the dock or her boat. But I'd been with her that morning. She called me to have breakfast with her, to let me down easy, and she'd told me about the engagement, showed me the ring. I was flabbergasted and confused, and she admitted to using me. Young and stupid, I argued that she loved me, but she disabused me of that notion really quickly. She loved Alex. I had been a pawn. I felt like an idiot." He met her gaze. "I *was* an idiot. Then I heard she'd been killed driving her boat recklessly, and I fell into a depression so deep I thought I'd never come out. Not just because she was dead but because I was so crazy about her that I didn't see she was using me. It was humbling and humiliating because the story got around really quickly. I left Xaviera. Hell, I left Europe. I came back to New York, licking my wounds and vowed it would never happen again. None of it."

"I'm sorry."

He sniffed a laugh. "You had your wake-up call with the boyfriend who wanted an in with your princess, but mine was a lot costlier. A lot harder to handle. In some respects, I don't think you ever recover when someone so young dies."

"No, you don't. I'm starting the school project because of a friend who died. The schools were her dream."

He frowned. "Your schools are someone else's idea?"

She nodded. "Yes." The limo pulled up to the curb outside her hotel. Kristen continued anyway.

"Aasera lived in Iraq. Her brothers were educated but she wasn't. She begged them to teach her to read and write and they did. She said it opened up a whole new world for her and she decided that she wanted to create schools for girls."

"And you picked up her crusade?"

"After she was killed by a suicide bomber."

"Oh, I'm sorry." Dean reached across and took her hand. "There aren't a lot of people who can say they understand and really mean it." He held her gaze. "But I do."

She could see in the depths of his dark eyes that he did understand, and she felt another one of those clicks of connection. This one more important than attraction or likes and dislikes. They'd both suffered a tragedy that had changed them. It was no wonder she kept feeling they meshed.

"I do this to honor her, but also because knowing her, hearing about her dream, I learned how important it was." She shrugged. "Her cause is now my cause."

The shrill sound of Dean's phone invaded the quiet. He winced. "It's the one I have to answer."

She nodded, glad for a few seconds to pull herself together before they said goodbye. Because this was it. They no longer had a reason to stay together. She'd gone to his party and lunch and both were over. Winslow Osmond wanted him to take his team to Grennady, but he didn't see the value in doing that. This time tomorrow he'd go back to being the ruthless businessman he always was and she'd be home, getting ready to step onto the world's stage as a founder of an organization that built schools.

After she got out of this limo, she'd never see him again.

Dean clicked the button to answer his phone. "Dean Suminski." He paused for a few seconds, then said, "Mrs. Flannigan. What a pleasant surprise. What can I do for you?"

He paused as the older woman talked. Suddenly feeling awful, missing Aasera, confused by all these feelings she had around Dean, Kristen buttoned her coat and slid across the seat to the limo door. Why prolong the inevitable? She barely knew him, and what she'd discovered only proved he was married to his business. And, really, she should be okay with their parting. She'd need all her mental and emotional energy to start her charity. Neither one of them had time for the other. Why belabor the issue with a goodbye in a busy hotel lobby?

Just when she would have opened the limo door, Dean caught her hand again.

"We'd love to. Seven tomorrow. We're looking forward to it."

She faced him as he clicked off the call. Though she hated the way her breath stuttered when he held her hand, happiness filled her at the possibility that this wasn't goodbye.

"You have another event?"

"Yes and no. *We've* been invited to a private dinner with the Flannigans." He smiled. His dark eyes lit with pleasure. "She wants to talk to *you* about your schools. Tomorrow night at seven."

CHAPTER SEVEN

"OH, MY GOSH! She wants to talk to *me*?"

Kristen looked at him, her stunning green eyes wide with excitement and he laughed. "You'll do fine." She drew in a long breath. "I had a few hiccups in my confidence today." She caught his gaze. "But you helped a lot."

A wave a pleasure flowed through him, but he didn't let himself wallow in it. He might be with Kristen for another party, but he wouldn't indulge the emotions he experienced around her. Especially the relief he'd felt sharing his story about Nina. Not because he didn't like the feelings she inspired in him, he did. He liked them too much. Keeping his distance was for *her* protection.

"Here's what we'll do. We'll have Stella take you shopping tomorrow morning to get you an appropriate dress."

She gasped. "She's going to have to take me

some place inexpensive! I can't afford the clothes in Jennifer's boutique."

He shook his head. "Whether you understand it or not, this dinner tomorrow night also works for me. While you talk with Mrs. Flannigan, I get a chance to chitchat with Arthur. She might own the business, but he's got influence over her." He smiled. "Actually, I owe you for the fact that your charity is getting me extra time with them."

"You just won't let this go, will you?"

"Not if you're about to pay for things that are helping me out." Deciding the time for teasing was over, he sucked in a breath. "Seriously. Thank you. I need this extra time with them, and you and your charity are providing it."

"Well, the dinner is supposed to be for me so I'm getting benefit too. That means there'll be no more agreements drawn up."

He drew a cross on his chest. "I promise."

Still in the limo, they placed a call to Jennifer at the boutique. Dean told her they needed a cocktail dress for the following night, and that Kristen would be in the next morning to look for one with Stella.

"Anything special I should pull for her to try on?"

"Just something pretty. We trust your judgment." He caught Kristen's gaze and smiled. "And make it red."

Kristen laughed as he clicked off the call. "Very funny."

"I'm getting much better at being funny."

She said, "You are," as Dean pressed the button for the chauffeur, who came around and opened the door.

Kristen got out and he followed behind her. He walked her into the hotel lobby and almost escorted her to her room, but the feelings he'd been having around her all day kept growing. Now they were committed to another evening out. He needed the time with the Flannigans as much as Kristen did—so he couldn't pass up this chance.

But as he spoke with Mrs. Minerva Flannigan about dinner Sunday night, he'd had the oddest sense they really were becoming a couple, and though he knew it wasn't true, there was a part of him that wished it was.

That was the real reason he couldn't walk her upstairs. He knew as surely as he knew his own name that if she gave him any sort of encouragement at all he'd kiss her. And then what?

Date?

Marry her?

The vision he'd had of him and Kristen in his master bedroom at his house in Albany filled his brain, and his chest tightened. How could he picture himself with a child when he had no clue how to be a father? How could he picture himself with someone as wonderful as Kristen when he was a stodgy workaholic who would get so involved in his projects and his business that he sometimes slept in his office?

How could he get involved with Kristen when he knew it would end…and knew, quite painfully, how paralyzing it was when a relationship ended. Nina might have died, but when she broke it off with him she'd outlined a hundred reasons they were wrong for each other, crushing his soul, reinforcing his beliefs that he shouldn't get involved in a real relationship.

His feelings for Kristen were wrong. He would stop them.

The elevator came. She stepped in and waved goodbye as the door closed, and he got back into the limo and headed for the sanctuary of his penthouse.

The limo stopped at his building, and he slid out and walked toward the glass revolving door, noticing an odd number of paparazzi hanging around. They came to attention when they saw him. One or two even snapped a picture. But neither of those things was unusual. First, the flirtatious daughter of a hedge fund manager lived in his building and she was a tabloid darling. Paparazzi were always around. Second, those who snapped pictures probably wanted a new file photo of him. God knew, there was nothing interesting about him walking into his building alone.

He breezed through the lobby, pausing only to say hello to the doorman. He used his code to get the private elevator to start and in a few seconds the door opened on his penthouse.

The whole place had been done in black and

white, with berry-toned throw pillows and accent pieces. He wouldn't know a berry tone from a hole in the ground, but his decorator had told him that berry colors were all the rage, so that's what he'd gotten.

He ambled into his bedroom and the walk-in closet, and chose black boots, blue jeans and an oatmeal-colored sweater, the color of which he also wouldn't have known if Stella hadn't told him when she showed him the array of sweaters she'd chosen for him that winter.

He didn't know fashionable colors. He didn't put his own touches on his houses and condos because he didn't really have homes. He had places he stayed. He was cold. Emotionless. And that was reason number seven hundred and forty-one why a nice woman like Kristen should stay away from him.

It was also reason number one that Nina had said she could never fall in love with him. Never really want to be with him.

He was cold. Not heartless. Just distanced from the world because of his genius and the way he was raised. He really didn't know how to connect.

Not wanting to think about Nina or Kristen anymore, and the yearning for something he knew he couldn't have, he grabbed the four newspapers he had delivered every morning.

Sitting on his sofa, he rifled through until he got to the *New York City Guardian*. He flipped it open but one section popped out and slid to the floor. The society pages. Without thought, he bent to pick it up, but there on the front page, bigger than was comfortable, was a picture of him and Kristen.

And he was laughing.

The photo itself confused him, reminding him of how differently he behaved with her. He slowly brought the paper up from the floor, staring at the picture first, then reading the caption.

Is the Iceman of Suminski Stuff falling in love?

His gut clenched. His gaze jumped to the article that detailed the troubles with his company and the article in *Tech Junkie*.

Crap.

But the worst were the closing lines.

Could the confirmed bachelor billionaire be dating someone? We doubt it. He has enough money that he doesn't have to meet women the old-fashioned way.

If innuendos could kill, he'd be dead right now. They'd all but suggested he'd hired Kristen.

And he had.

He dropped his head to his hands, then called his driver and told him to be in front of the building in ten minutes. After slipping into his black leather bomber jacket and gloves, he scooped the paper off his sofa before heading for the elevator.

Outside his building, as his limo pulled up and he raced to the door, the whir of cameras followed him.

Damn it.

In the bathroom of her suite, Kristen stood in the fluffy white robe debating. Shower or bubble bath? The room came equipped with any supplies she could possibly need, and though the shower gel was nice, the bubble bath crystals smelled divine. It was a sinful, wonderful, guilty pleasure to have the rest of the afternoon and all of the evening to herself to do what she wanted, and she was taking full advantage.

She chose the bubble bath, started the water and poured in the crystals, which instantly became iridescent foam. Immersed in bubbles, she closed her eyes. Unfortunately, as she sank into the water she thought about Dean.

After hearing his story about Nina, she realized she knew *nothing* about being used. Brad was a man who wanted money and power, and he did what he had to do to get it. Unashamedly. Almost embarrassingly obviously. If Kristen had opened her eyes, she'd have easily seen it.

But using an inexperienced nineteen-year-old to make another boyfriend jealous? Kristen couldn't even imagine what Dean had felt when Nina had told him. It was no wonder he had so much pride. And no wonder he disliked mixing business with pleasure, given that it was Nina's father who had set them up as a condition to giving Dean money.

It was perfectly understandable that the situation had scarred him. This also explained his need for agreements and rules. She actually admired him for pulling himself together as much as he had. In the years that followed Nina and her father using him, and a world leader hating him, Dean had built an empire.

So she couldn't feel sorry for him. He certainly didn't feel sorry for himself. But she also couldn't stop herself from coupling his difficult beginnings—losing his parents, being raised by a grandmother who didn't want him—to being publicly humiliated when he tried to get funding.

It was no wonder he not only noticed but understood when her confidence wobbled.

Sunk neck-deep in bubbles, she almost cursed when the phone rang. Not sure who it might be, since she'd called her parents and given them her hotel room number in case anything happened, she got out of the tub, slid into the fluffy terry cloth robe and grabbed the extension in the bathroom.

"Yes."

"It's me. Dean. Can I come up?"

She grimaced. "Now?"

"It's important."

"Okay. I'm just getting out of the tub. Give me five minutes."

She hastily dried, dressed in the jeans and red sweater he'd bought for her to wear home, and combed out her hair. Because it was an unruly mass, she twisted it into a bun before she walked into the sitting room. A few seconds later, there was a knock on her door.

Expecting Dean, she opened it.

He handed a newspaper to her. "I'm sorry."

She glanced down at it and saw it was folded to display a picture of them printed on the first page of that section.

"Oh-oh."

"It's not a big deal, except they suggest that I hired you to date me."

She laughed. "They're sort of right."

"Yes. They are." He ambled into her sitting room. "We have a written agreement that proves it."

She really liked the way he looked in the leather jacket and boots. Though a suit gave him an air of power, the jacket, jeans and boots made him look strong, male, virile.

She pulled back from that train of thought before she had to fan herself. "So we have an argreement? No one will see it."

He scrubbed his hand down his face. "No, no one will see it. But this is the kind of gossip I don't need when my company's in trouble."

"Really? I don't understand how it relates."

"I look like a lunatic."

Because she'd just run through all the attributes of how he "looked" she thoroughly disagreed. But even though Kristen herself never had to worry about the press, Princess Eva did. Like it or not, think it was funny or not, Kristen understood.

"You know, you didn't hire me for tomorrow night's dinner."

He sucked in a breath. "So?"

"So it kind of, sort of, is a real date."

His eyes narrowed. "What are you getting at?"

"Well, if we went out—right now for instance, when, again, you're not paying me—and saw some sights and then got dinner, we would officially be dating."

"And if someone saw us—like the photographers following me—then we'd look official."

She shook her head. "No. Get into the spirit of this. We won't *look* official. We *will be* dating."

He met her gaze. "Oh."

She sighed. "Thanks for your enthusiastic response."

"I'm sorry. I just don't date."

"And you wonder why the press prints crazy articles about you?"

He laughed.

She smiled. "See? Dating me is not so bad. Especially since I come with a shelf life. I have to go home sometime."

"No ugly breakup."

"Exactly."

He pondered that for a second before he said, "Grab your coat. We're going to Rockefeller Center."

Since she was wearing jeans, she got her old black wool coat from the closet by the door. "Sounds promising."

"Every tourist goes there. They have a big Christmas tree."

"Fun!"

He pulled in a breath. "I suppose."

Kristen shook her head, but didn't scold him about being a Scrooge. Knowing his story, she could easily see why all this would be new to him.

Out on the sidewalk, a couple of guys in winter jackets—trying to be inconspicuous about holding cameras—followed them to Rockefeller Center. Obviously, they were members of the press Dean was so worried about.

She didn't have to point them out. She was fairly certain Dean saw them, but he pretended he didn't. So she pretended too. When he started talking about her charity, she let him.

"You're going to need a board of advisors."

She skipped along the sidewalk, working to keep up with his long strides. A light snow began to fall, and she inhaled deeply, suddenly homesick for fresh snow, her mom's homemade gingerbread cookies and the way the sun dipped at about three in the afternoon, making the world a silent, peaceful place. Even on a Saturday, New York City was mad, noisy, filled with life and energy.

"I know I'll need advisors. In fact, I'm counting on advisors helping me through the things I don't know."

"If Mrs. Flannigan ponies up anything over five hundred grand, it will be a subtle indicator that she wants on that board."

She stopped walking. "Five hundred thousand dollars?"

He shrugged. "As I said, she might be angling for a seat on that board. I'd give it to her."

"You better believe I will."

Her silly answer made him laugh and she slid her arm beneath his to nestle against him, whispering, "This is for authenticity."

He glanced down at her. "Oh."

Their gazes held. His dark orbs held a wisp of longing that tugged at her soul, but he said nothing. So she took that for agreement and stayed close as they made the few blocks' walk to Rockefeller Center.

When she saw the enormous Christmas tree, she gasped. "It's beautiful."

Decorated with multicolored lights, the huge tree was festive and happy, and again filled Kristen with a longing for home. She knew she'd be back in Grennady for the holidays, but right now she was missing all the fun of prepping. All the cookie baking. All the decorating.

"This tree is why Rockefeller Center is a big tourist attraction."

She saw people ice-skating in the huge sectioned-off center. Her longing for home doubled. "There's skating!"

"That's reason two that this is a tourist attraction."

"Do you count everything?"

His head tilted in confusion. "Count?"

"Keep track."

He laughed. "I suppose I do. I think it's the way my brain files things."

She said, "Interesting," but her attention was again caught by the skaters. The snow picked up, but she didn't feel cold. Having grown up in a Scandinavian country, she was more than accustomed to snow and temperatures much colder than what New York City offered. The swish, swish, swish of the skaters as they whirled by filled her with homesickness.

"I think we should skate."

He blanched. "No way in hell."

"Why not?" She glanced at him and the leather jacket over his warm sweater and jeans. "We're both dressed for it. There's a sign over there that says they rent skates." She bumped his shoulder with her own. "It'll be fun."

"Not with three reporters following us. I do not want a bunch of guys with access to important media outlets to see me fall on my ass. I don't want to look like an idiot."

"You won't look like an idiot. You'll look like someone who likes me enough to try something new. Then speculation will go from 'did he pay her?' to 'who is this woman who has him trying new things?'"

He shook his head. "You know they're about to investigate you, right?"

She shrugged. "You did."

He sighed.

"And what did you find? That I'm a nice, simple girl. Your search didn't hurt me. Didn't affect me. So I let it go." She smiled. "Not everything has to be life-or-death. Let's just have fun. The photographers following you will see that. They'll investigate me and find nothing and poof they'll disappear."

"You're such an optimist."

She turned to him and studied his face. "You know, I'd say you're a pessimist but I don't think that's true. I think so many crappy things happened to you that you're just careful."

"Careful enough not to break my ankle."

"See? There you go. Deflecting again because that's how you stay away from subjects that are too painful. But you don't have to worry. I won't ask you to talk about Nina anymore. I won't ask about your childhood. But I do want to skate. I'm in a new country unexpectedly, for longer than I thought, and I'm just a little homesick."

If she'd argued or tried to get her own way, Dean would have easily beaten her. But what kind of a Scrooge would he have to be to deny her the chance to get over her homesickness?

He sighed. "I'll check out the skating schedule and see about skate rental."

Her entire face brightened. "Really?"

"Yes. But don't think I'm trying anything fancy. And no holding my hand."

"We're supposed to be dating."

"I don't want to look weak on the ice."

With that he walked away. Because it was an odd time of the day, they could actually get into the next round of skating. He called her over. They rented skates. Within twenty minutes they were on the ice.

After a few minutes of wobbling, working to get his balance, knowing photographers were documenting his efforts, Dean finally found his footing. The first time he glided along for more than a few feet, he burst out laughing.

"All right. It's fun."

She skated a circle around him. "I told you."

"You actually use the same core muscles to balance yourself as you do for snowboarding."

She gaped at him. "You snowboard?"

"Used to. I had to learn to do a lot of things to be in the places where I could accidentally run into the wealthy people I thought most likely to invest in Suminski Stuff."

"You make me feel like I should be grateful Mrs. Flannigan invited me to dinner."

He stopped skating. "You should."

"I am."

Silence stretched between them as they studied each other. Skaters glided around them, reminding him that he was stopped, staring at her, taking in that earnest face and those beautiful eyes, and reporters were probably noticing.

She quickly caught his hand and pulled him into the fray. "Let's get out of everybody's way, and then I'll drop your hand."

He almost wished she wouldn't. The connection to her felt so nice, so normal, that it should have scared him. Instead, it filled him with the sense that he could trust her to take him places he'd never been.

They skated into a rhythm and she dropped his hand, but he scooped hers up again.

Her gaze flew to his.

"We are supposed to be dating."

She nodded and smiled as she skated in front of him. "Wanna do a trick?"

"Getting bored with just plain skating?"

"Sort of. But I also think I'd rather get my picture in the paper for doing something cool, than for looking like two spectators who didn't know what they were doing."

He laughed nervously. "Seriously? You're going to make me do a trick?"

"A simple one." She grabbed his other hand so they stood facing each other, both hands tightly clasped. Then she shifted them so they were skating sideways and that movement became a circle.

He imagined that from the spectator area they looked cute, fun. And they probably did pose a much better picture. But as the world whizzed by and he grew more comfortable, with her and with his skates, he started to laugh. For the first time in weeks, he wasn't thinking about his company or his troubles. He wasn't thinking at all.

Except to realize that he really did trust her.

* * *

Kristen noticed the change in him immediately. She stopped their circle and dropped one of his hands so she could pull him behind her. When they got enough speed, she led him into a figure eight.

He called, "Now I think you're showing off."

"Nope. Showing off would be teaching you how to do a spin or maybe a lift."

She expected his face to freeze in horror. Instead, he said, "I could probably spin."

She pulled him out of their third figure eight and guided him to stand beside her. "You like being good at things."

"Don't you?"

She shrugged. "I like doing the best I can."

"Same thing."

She said, "I suppose," but she understood what he meant. As a genius, his version of doing the best he could undoubtedly meant that he had to be perfect. It was why he didn't want to fall on his face in front of reporters, why he stayed out of the public eye. People were always watching him. Maybe hoping he'd make a mistake.

When their ninety minutes were up, they left Rockefeller Center, walked a bit more around that section of the city and had dinner at an out-of-the-way Mexican restaurant.

She buttoned her jacket as they walked out onto the now snow-covered sidewalk. Christmas lights decorated shop-front windows and doorways. Snow sat on evergreen branches like icing on sugar cookies. Without hesitation, he took her hand and she couldn't stop a smile.

It was one of the best dates of her life.

Still, she knew it didn't mean as much to him as it did to her. He might be having fun. He might even be enjoying her, but having heard the story of Nina, she more than suspected he'd vowed never to let himself get close to a woman again. He'd probably even made a rule.

When they reached her hotel lobby, she expected him to say goodbye at the elevator. Instead, he stepped inside with her.

Wonderful hope filled her tummy with butterflies. "Walking me to my door?"

"There were three photographers in the lobby."

Disappointment rumbled through her. "Oh."

But when they got to her door and she turned to say good-night, he had the most baffling expression on his face. She recognized the longing. The end of this date should be a kiss. But the confusion in his eyes told her he wouldn't even kiss her cheek.

"What's wrong?"

He drew a long breath and looked away. "Nothing." But when he turned back to her again, his dark eyes had sharpened. The muscles of his broad shoulders tensed beneath his smooth leather jacket. He took a fraction of a step toward her.

Her breath stalled. He *was* going to kiss her.

She took a fraction of a step toward him, drawn by an unknown instinct inside her that seemed to know exactly what to do.

His eyes stayed on her face. One of his hands came up, as if he were going to put it on her shoulder or maybe her waist to nudge her closer.

Her heart did a rumba in her chest. She smiled hopefully.

But his hand stopped. He took a step back and ran his fingers through his hair.

"Good night."

Disappointed, she whispered, "Good night," but he just stood there. She thought for a second that he might be hanging around because he didn't want to leave and did want to kiss her. Then she realized he was just being a gentleman, waiting for her to go into her room.

She quickly slid the key in the lock and let herself inside. She said, "Good night," again, hoping she didn't look like an idiot, then closed the door behind her.

But no matter how hard she tried to talk herself out of it, she couldn't let herself believe it was okay that he didn't kiss her.

She had wanted him to kiss her.

Very much.

She told herself that was trouble, reminded herself of his story of Nina and how her now favorite genius had probably made a rule to protect himself, and even suggested to herself that no matter how they manipulated this agreement of theirs, they were using each other.

But she still wanted him to kiss her.

CHAPTER EIGHT

"DEAN TOLD ME you need a cocktail dress and that I'm to take you to lunch."

Eyes squinting, Kristen eyed the time on her cell phone and saw it was already ten o'clock.

She sat up. "Yes. I'm sorry, Stella. I got up late or I'd be dressed by now."

"No sweat. I'm in the lobby when you're ready."

"Thanks."

Kristen got out of bed, showered and put on the red sweater and jeans again. Then she called the front desk and made arrangements to have her black pants, white shirt and underwear cleaned that day. Housekeeping promised her clothes would be back in her room by that evening and she thanked them. Now there'd be no arguments about how she "needed" more jeans and a new sweater. She would fly home in the clothes she'd been wearing in Paris.

She met Stella in the lobby. They took Dean's limo to the boutique and found Jennifer waiting, ready with three red cocktail dresses. She tried on all three and chose a simple red lace sheathe.

Stella said, "Now we just need new jeans and sweater."

Proud of herself, Kristen smirked and said, "For what?"

"Dean said something about you needing clothes to go home in."

"The clothes I wore over from Paris are being cleaned by the hotel." She smiled. "I'm fine."

Stella gaped at her. "Are you nuts? The man is willing to buy you an eight-hundred-dollar sweater. Take it."

"I don't need it."

Stella sighed and looked at the ceiling as if seeking guidance from above.

Kristen firmly said, "I don't need it and I don't want it. End of discussion."

Shaking her head, Stella said, "Whatever."

They had Jennifer send the red dress to her hotel and left the boutique for a restaurant.

The snow from the day before had been shoveled away, but steam rose from the grates in the sidewalk, mixing with the frigid air and swirling toward street vendors who stood huddled by food carts.

"Where do you want to eat?"

She pointed at one of the carts. "A hot dog would be fine."

"No. Dean said to get you a proper meal."

Kristen laughed. "He's probably the bossiest guy I've ever met."

Stella snorted. "You don't know the half of it." She pointed at the door of an Italian restaurant. "Do you like Italian?"

"Everybody likes Italian."

"Great." They took the three steps down into the lower-level restaurant and found there was no wait.

Seated at the round table, holding her menu, Stella said, "So you're okay with another date?"

"Are you asking for Dean or are you curious?"

Stella leaned forward. "Dean sounded as if he believed you were perfectly happy with tonight's dinner. That's what makes me curious."

"The dinner is actually for me. Mrs. Flannigan wants to talk about my charity."

Stella peered over her menu. "Well, good, then. Dean's a difficult man even for pretend dates. I'm glad to see you're getting something out of this deal."

"You mean aside from a gown, two dresses, a sweater, jeans, boots, a black coat and two pairs of black heels." She paused, then cursed. "Damn it! He still hasn't taken back that bracelet."

Stella laughed. "Lighten up. To Dean that's not even pocket change."

The waiter, a short Italian man who must have come directly from Italy because he spoke with a wonderful accent, took their orders.

As he scampered away, Kristen refused to let the subject of the bracelet die. "I've got to get that bracelet back to him."

Stella leaned forward again. "Why do you care? The man's a surly bastard. He fires employees and drops lovers like the rest of us change shoes. The only person he really talks to is Jason."

"He talks to me."

Stella gasped. "Oh." She considered that for a second, then gasped again. "Oh, no! I think I see what's going on here." She shook her head fiercely. "Sweetie, do not let that man get his hooks into you. You are too nice of a girl. And if you really want to start that charity you told me about the other day, you can't have your reputation sullied by having dated Dean."

Annoyed, Kristen said, "First of all, he's not that bad. From what I saw at the Christmas party and our lunch with his friends, he talks when he has something to say. At yesterday's lunch he was a virtual chatty Cathy. Second, dating one guy isn't going to ruin my business reputation."

Stella put her elbow on the table and rested her head on her closed fist. "Okay, I take the reputation thing back. And change it to the reality that he *could* ruin you with a broken heart. He is as hard-nosed as a businessman gets. Do not let a few nights out fool you into thinking he's nice or he likes you."

Fiddling with her napkin, Kristen said, "I'm not that stupid." But she'd wanted him to kiss her the night before. Really wanted it. And from everything Stella was saying, she didn't know him. She had been dealing with a guy who was at first grouchy, then standoffish, then nicer and nicer, more open, willing to take a risk ice-skating. A guy who was either growing comfortable with her or changing...or something.

The picture of Dean, sitting in the limo beside her, saying, *Maybe you bring out the best in me*, popped into her head.

What if she did bring out the best in him?

But what if she didn't? What if he really was a snarky guy who needed her, so he was acting the way he had to, to keep her here in New York, available for appearances at his beck and call?

Oh, that made so much more sense than to think a farm girl from Grennady could tame the New York City genius superstar.

When Dean came to Kristen's hotel room to pick her up at seven, she was ready to go. Wearing a red lace dress, with her yellow hair swirling around her in big, loose curls, she looked amazing.

But he'd almost kissed her the night before, so

tempted he nearly lost the war inside his head, even though he knew kissing her was wrong. They had a deal. They weren't really dating in spite of the fact that they'd set it up to look that way. He could not kiss her.

Tonight, he would be smarter.

He picked up her black wool coat from the back of the sofa and opened it so she could slide it on.

"Thank you."

Was it just him, or had that thank-you seemed a little clipped?

He opened the door for her. She stepped into the hall. "Thanks again."

That one was definitely stiff, too polite. Not Kristen at all.

"You're welcome." He paused, then said, "Is something wrong?"

"I'm fine."

She wasn't fine.

"Did Stella say something?"

The elevator arrived. They stepped inside. Standing face forward, Kristen said, "Stella and I had a great time."

"Well, you certainly picked out a nice dress."

"Jennifer picked it."

The chill of her voice and the way she wouldn't look at him sent a sprinkle of apprehension up his spine. Stella could have told her a million things, all of which would make Kristen back off.

But she should back off. He didn't date. He took lovers. She didn't fit that category. She'd be wise not to get close to him.

And he would be wise to let her do whatever it was she felt she needed to do to protect herself.

They drove to the Flannigans' in complete silence, and, for once, it felt odd. He almost pointed out the decorated storefront windows, remembering how she'd loved the Christmas tree in Rockefeller Center, but held back, respecting her obvious wish to keep her distance. But the more he held his tongue, the more the decorations popped out to him. Fat Santas in store windows. Elves. Bright Christmas ornaments. He hadn't really looked at decorations since the year his grandmother gave him fifty bucks and told him to buy himself a gift. She didn't want to decorate. Didn't want to bake. Didn't want to go out at all. Because Christmas was a holiday created by stores to get people to spend money.

So he'd taken his fifty bucks to a pawnshop and bought some poor sap's old computer. To stave off the sadness of missing his parents and wishing Christmas was real, he told himself his grandmother was right. Christmas was a sham. For foolish people who could be duped.

The limo pulled up to the Flannigans' building. Dean and Kristen said nothing walking into the building lobby, nothing as the doorman—who had them on an expected-visitors list—walked them to the elevator and used a key card to allow the elevator to take them to the upper floor and the Flannigan residence.

As the elevator opened on the stunning foyer and a beaming Mrs. Flannigan and Arthur, Dean started to sweat, worried how Kristen's unhappiness might affect the evening. And her charity. If she was quiet with Mrs. Flannigan, the potential donation could go sailing out the window.

Worse, it was his fault because Stella had probably told her he was a bastard.

Because he was.

She stepped out of the elevator into Mrs. Flannigan's hug. "Let John take your coats."

As Mrs. Flannigan said the words, her butler stepped forward for Kristen's black wool coat and Dean's charcoal-gray overcoat.

As Kristen slid out of hers, Mrs. Flannigan gasped. "Oh, red! You look so lovely in red. I remember those days. I used to love to wear red."

Kristen laughed. "Used to? I'm sure you're still stunning in red."

Mrs. Flannigan hooked her arm through Kristen's and led her down a long hall, into a high-ceilinged living room replete with art. Furnished with simple ultramodern sofas and chairs, the room got its beauty from famous paintings hung on walls and sculptures scattered about. Red velvet bows and evergreen branches hung over paintings, a nod to the holiday.

Kristen said, "Your home is lovely."

"Thank you. Some people," she said, her gaze sliding to Dean, "use decorators. I prefer to make my home my home."

Though Mrs. Flannigan and Arthur looked at him, Kristen kept her gaze averted.

She did that the whole way through dinner, through the discussion of her charity and the promise of a sizable donation from Mrs. Flannigan. Kristen mentioned inviting her onto her board of advisors, and, as Dean had predicted, her eyes sparkled with approval as she happily accepted the position and volunteered to find other board members.

"Who will also make donations," Mrs. Flannigan promised. She tossed out a few names, people famous enough to make even Dean's head spin, but when that discussion was over she turned to Dean.

"Now that our real business is out of the way, I think you and I need to have a chat."

The way she looked at him sent fear rattling along his nerve endings. She had too much life and energy to remind him of his grandmother, but she was so influential on Wall Street that one word from her could send his stock into a free fall.

Seated on her sofa, with after-dinner drinks,

he crossed one leg over the other and leaned back on the cushion as if totally unconcerned.

"So chat."

"Winslow was right about you taking your staff somewhere now—right now—to motivate them to get this project done. I've had my assistant investigate Grennady and it's quiet. Peaceful. But the country still has enough things for your employees and their families to do that it could be like a working vacation."

"It sounds great, but—"

"No buts, Dean. This time next month my word isn't going to be enough to stave off the inevitable."

"I know that."

"So you have no choice but to try something different."

"I'm just not convinced that taking them out of their work environment will jump-start their creativity."

"Look at it this way, keeping them where they are hasn't worked in three years. I'm going to be bold enough to suggest that you have nothing to lose."

Kristen unexpectedly reached out and took his hand. It shocked him that she'd think he'd need support for what was, essentially, a simple business conversation. Then he realized how sweet it was—especially considering that she'd been protecting herself all night.

When she thought he needed her, she was there for him.

No one had ever been there for him.

It didn't matter that she mistakenly believed Mrs. Flannigan's stern voice somehow cowed him. It hadn't. No one cowed him. What mattered was she took his feelings into consideration over her own.

An indescribable feeling invaded his chest. A warmth that rose until it filled his blood and every happiness-starved cell in his body.

All the feelings he'd had skating returned. Especially the sense that his world was opening up and he could trust her.

He couldn't follow the feeling. He wouldn't risk hurting Kristen. But for once in his life he wanted to soak it in.

The conversation shifted to a painting over the

marble fireplace. Kristen and Mrs. Flannigan walked over to it, with Mrs. Flannigan telling the story behind the purchase.

Though he spoke with Arthur, Dean let his gaze follow Kristen around the room, knowing she wasn't faking her interest in the art, or her immediate love of Mrs. Flannigan.

And he suddenly, desperately wanted to kiss her. Even more desperately than he had the night before.

The evening wound down. As they made their way up the hall toward the foyer with the elevator, John approached them, holding their coats. Dean helped Kristen with hers before putting on his own.

"Oh, look at this," Mrs. Flannigan said, pointing at a huge spray of flowers on the hall table. "You're not exactly under the mistletoe in that arrangement, but you're beside it." She nudged Dean. "If you wanted to kiss her, Arthur and I wouldn't mind."

A rush of need swooshed through Dean's bloodstream. It was the perfectly logical way to get the kiss he'd wanted for nearly two days.

He'd already vowed he wouldn't get involved with her, wouldn't hurt her...but didn't he deserve one kiss?

Of course he did.

Kristen laughed. "Mistletoe has to be overhead for it to be a legitimate reason to get a kiss."

Then she strode toward the elevator, Mrs. Flannigan following behind, chuckling, and Arthur behind his wife.

Dean glanced at the flower arrangement, then looked up at the group, all of whom had their backs to him. And he did something he had never done. He pilfered some mistletoe.

In the limo, Kristen went back to being quiet. He let her because it was the right thing to do. They drove up Fifth Avenue, Christmas decorations glittering in the frigid night air, and he took a long drink of air. The same decorations that had reminded him of his past twinkled in the light of the streetlamps and unexpectedly warmed his heart, even as apprehension tugged at his soul.

His time with Kristen was almost at an end.

And he had some decisions to make in the few minutes left of their drive to her hotel.

He debated a couple of things, but in the end, he knew Mrs. Flannigan was simply too powerful to ignore. He was going to have to take his staff to Grennady. He fingered the mistletoe in his overcoat pocket. But to keep things simple and protect Kristen, he also had to cut Kristen out of the picture.

They got out of the limo and for the first time in two days there was no paparazzi following them.

Kristen noticed too. "No press?"

"It's late and cold, and we gave them enough pictures yesterday to keep them happy."

She said, "Ah," as he held open the door for her.

They walked to the elevator in total silence and waited for it to arrive in equal silence.

She gave him a confused look when he followed her inside, but he said nothing. When the elevator reached her floor, he walked out with her, staying as quiet as they had in the limo.

At the door, she turned to him with a polite

smile. "Thank you very much for this evening. Heck, thanks for introducing me to Mrs. Flannigan. She's wonderful. Perfect. I know that with her help my charity will be up and running in about half the time it would have taken me alone."

He smiled. "Probably even less than that. She's very powerful." He smiled again. "And she likes you."

"I like her too."

Pride for her surged through him. Not because she was great, but because she was honest. She genuinely liked Mrs. Flannigan, and with her assistance Kristen probably would changes the lives of hundreds of thousands of women, maybe millions, over her lifetime.

"You'll make a good team."

"Thanks."

For the first time all night, she looked him in the eye. The effect was instantaneous. Dean's heart swelled again. His breath froze in his lungs.

And he knew this had to be the last time he

saw her. If he let her stay in his life, he wouldn't be able to resist this pull.

Digging her key card out of her purse, she said, "I'll be in touch when it comes time for the computers."

"Good."

She turned to open her door, but he stopped her. "Not so fast, Cinderella. You want me and my company in Grennady, and it looks like you've got us there."

Her eyes widened. "Really?"

"You heard what Mrs. Flannigan said."

She frowned. "Yes, but everybody's been saying that and you didn't appear to have taken any of them seriously."

"Mrs. Flannigan's a brilliant businesswoman. And she wields a lot of power. Not taking her advice would be like asking her to downgrade my stock."

"So you're moving your company to Grennady?"

"Temporarily. If my staff can finish this project before the first of the year, I will consider a permanent move."

"But that's three weeks! And Christmas is in there!"

"Yeah. Bad luck for you. If I were you, I'd be on the phone tonight, finding office space. And I hope you have a strategy for handling Prince Alex because once we get to Grennady I'll be dealing exclusively with the royal family."

That was how he planned to circumvent his unwanted feelings around Kristen. He would simply push her out of his life by working only with King Mason or Princess Eva. He had it all figured out.

But that didn't mean he didn't recognize that something wonderful was passing him by. He'd never before felt the way he felt around her. He knew he wasn't made for what she wanted or needed. But he also knew what he felt for her was special. *She* was special.

And he couldn't walk away without a kiss.

He fingered the chunk of mistletoe he'd taken from Mrs. Flannigan's huge display. His heartbeat slowed as his brain cleared. He deserved at least one kiss. He wasn't the guy who would get the girl. He wasn't a guy who was going to have a happily-ever-after—

But surely he was entitled to one little kiss from the first woman who made him think happily-ever-after might exist.

And even if he wasn't, he was taking one.

He pulled the mistletoe from his pocket. "You said this only works if it's overhead…right?"

Her gaze jumped to his.

He raised his arm, putting the mistletoe directly above them before he put his hand on her shoulder and stepped closer. Her eyes widened, but he didn't give her time to ponder or protest. He dipped his head and pressed his lips to hers.

CHAPTER NINE

SURPRISE AND INSTINCT caused Kristen to lift her lips and kiss him back. He took advantage and nudged a bit, encouraging her to open her mouth. When she did, he deepened the kiss and all the breath stalled in her lungs. His lips were smooth and sleek, his kiss experienced.

Desire whooshed through her. Her brain stopped. Wonderful urges spun through her. She shoved her hotel room key into her coat pocket, stepped closer and smoothed her hands up his silky shirt, over his shoulders until they met at his nape. Another half step eased her body against his chest.

It was heaven. As his hungry mouth took hers, and his hands slid down her back, then up again, the whole world slimmed down to just him and her, and spiraling sensations that made her feel dizzy and warm and just a little confused.

Then he broke the kiss and stepped back, away from her.

Kristen stared at him. Her heart beat crazily. Her thoughts sambaed. The mouth he'd just kissed so thoroughly couldn't form words.

"It was really nice to meet you, Kristen Anderson. Good luck with your charity. When the time comes, let Stella know and you'll have your computers."

She watched his long-legged stride take him down the hall to the elevator, her entire body shimmering.

The man had kissed her! And not like some soulless nerd, like a poet—a love-starved poet.

Her brain couldn't sort it out. He'd barely wanted to hold her hand the day before. He'd absolutely walked away from a kiss at this very same hotel room door. But tonight after she'd all but ignored him, he'd kissed her.

She didn't know what to think, except that his parting words were definitely a goodbye.

She tried not to read too much into the wistful way he'd said goodbye, and the puzzling sadness that tightened her throat as he turned a corner and disappeared from view. Each was for nothing. They both knew how this worked. No matter how attracted he might be to her, men like him didn't date ordinary girls.

They also didn't deal with assistants—even if said assistant was executive assistant to a princess. As he'd said, he'd be communicating with the royal family from here on out. When she needed her computers, she'd be talking with Stella. She'd never see or speak to him again.

She shook herself to force away the sadness that brought, and opened the door to her suite. If he and his staff planned to be in Grennady the next day, and he intended to communicate with the royal family, she couldn't spend her time wondering about a stupid kiss and a sexy, interesting, but patently unusual man. She had some calls to make.

She tossed her coat onto an available chair and found her phone. After calculating the time difference between midnight in New York and middle of the day in Xaviera, she dialed.

Princess Eva answered on the second ring. "Kristen?"

Eva's voice was soft and sweet, but there was a thread of steel that ran through it. She might be a wonderful person, but she was a future queen. A strong woman destined to rule a country.

"Please don't fire me."

"Fire you?" Eva laughed. "You're the best assistant I've ever had. What could you have possibly done to be fired?"

She took a long drink of air to steady her nerves, then said, "I've been watching you and Alex try to entice a tech company to Grennady."

"Yes."

"I also know your list had dwindled. There was no one left to contact."

"That's a subject we intend to revisit in January."

She swallowed. "Well, you may not have to. I approached Dean Suminski—"

"Of Suminski Stuff?"

"Yes."

"Oh, no! Alex hates him."

Kristen said, "I know."

"Then why would you approach him?"

"At the time, I didn't know Alex hated him. I

just thought maybe you and Alex didn't think we stood a chance with him."

"Oh, Kristen!"

She paced into the bedroom of the suite out of the area that reminded her of Dean helping her with her coat, talking about the press, and them deciding they could "date" for real. All of that was just so confusing. In a couple of days of being with Dean Suminski, she'd really grown to like him. But he didn't want anything to do with her.

Otherwise, he wouldn't be saying goodbye... would he?

"I'm so sorry. But I swear I didn't know there was bad blood between them until Dean told me when we were on our way to a Christmas party—"

"You went to a Christmas party with Dean Suminski? He's in Grennady?"

"No, we're in New York."

Eva gasped. "What are you doing in New York?"

"It is a long, long story, Princess." Kristen fell to the huge king-size bed, realizing how odd this whole thing sounded. But, one step at a time, it had all made sense.

Even her feelings for him.

Inch by inch, he'd shown himself to her, and inch by inch she'd fallen for the man she genuinely believed he was deep down inside.

"I'd intended to start this explanation off with an apology for overstepping, but I now know I more than overstepped. It just seemed wrong that we never approached Suminski Stuff. So I found Dean in Paris."

"Paris?"

"I called in a favor to get the name of his hotel, and he agreed to give me five minutes in the limo ride to his airstrip, but that didn't work out. So I was going to fly to New York to have time with him while we were in the air, but his friend was on the plane, waiting for him. He told Dean his stock was being downgraded." She sucked in a breath. "His company's in trouble. He intends to fix it. But he has to get his latest game series to beta testers the first of the year to prove Suminski Stuff is still viable. Anyway, we were having dinner tonight with Mrs. Flannigan, a woman who owns a huge brokerage firm, who told him to get his staff somewhere quiet and peaceful and get this project done."

"Dinner tonight? Are you dating this guy?"

She winced. "Yes." And it had been her idea because she hated the way everyone misinterpreted him, but more because she'd wanted to date him for real. She liked him.

"You may see it in a newspaper. So, yes, we were sort of dating. But we did it so the press wouldn't think he'd paid me to go to the Christmas party because he sort of had."

"Kristen!"

"It's not what you think. In exchange for me being his date for an important party, we signed an agreement for him to provide the first hundred-thousand-dollars' worth of computers when I start my schools."

Eva's voice softened. "So you're leaving us to start your charity?"

"That was the point of the dinner with Mrs. Flannigan—"

"Is this Minerva Flannigan?"

"Yes. She's the first of my board of advisors."

Eva's voice softened. "She's got a great business mind. She's the perfect choice to be on your board of advisors."

"And of course I want you on the board too, Princess."

Eva laughed. "My ego is not so fragile that you need to pamper me."

"But I really do want you on this board."

"Then I am honored."

"But I'm also not going anywhere yet. Dean Suminski and his staff will be in Grennady tomorrow evening, our time. He needs office space. Though I could easily get it for him if I had a couple of weeks, he needs it tomorrow and I don't have that kind of clout."

"Okay. Getting a company like Suminski Stuff into Grennady could be really good for us. Alex has been a ruler too long to let a ten-year-old problem keep him from doing the right thing, but that doesn't mean we'll poke the bear. As long as we keep Alex away from Dean Suminski everything should be fine."

"But he expects to be dealing with the royal family."

"And he will. He'll deal with me. I have some thoughts on how to get office space. So I'll make some calls." Princess Eva paused. "And, Kristen?"

"Yes?"

"Be careful with this guy."

Kristen laughed. "Right." But remembering the way he'd kissed her shot that odd longing through her—even though she knew he had no intention of seeing her again. The way he said goodbye proved that. And she should be glad. Rich guys didn't marry commoners. They used them. Hadn't one heartbreak been enough?

She was smarter than to long for something that made no sense.

"He's got to be the grouchiest man on the face of the earth. I think I'll be fine."

"So the accident changed him?"

"Accident?"

"Dean was a very happy sort of party guy, until Alex's girlfriend was killed after Dean—" Eva paused. Her tone went from conversational to royal in one indrawn breath. "Actually, Kristen, if Dean didn't tell you, then let's not poke that bear, either."

"He told me."

"Then you understand how sensitive this is."

"Yes, ma'am."

"I'll call in some favors to find Suminski office space. Our vacation is over in two days. There's no sense in cutting it short now. You can handle Dean and his staff for two days, right?"

Kristen said, "Yes, ma'am," again, but she hung up the phone with the oddest feeling in her stomach. Dean might think he wouldn't see her again, but Princess Eva had just put her in charge of him.

She tried to stem the crazy bubbly feeling behind her ribs, but she couldn't. Dean might seem like the coldest man on earth to the rest of the world, but he'd confided in her, laughed with her, kissed her.

She did not want to let him go.

Dean's jet landed in Grennady four hours after the plane carrying Kristen, Stella and the portion of Suminski Stuff staff who were working on the series of games. Jason was staying in New York to do some PR and some hand-holding, so Dean had met him for breakfast before he'd flown out. But he'd been glad to have the excuse of meeting Jason, so he didn't have to spend a long flight with Kristen, tempted by another kiss, wishing circumstances in his life were different. Because his life wasn't different. It couldn't be different. He was who he was.

And damn it! Though he'd had a rough beginning and made one huge mistake involving Alexandros Sancho, he was basically a lucky guy. Mostly because that mistake with Alexandros had taught him some hard lessons. He now did nothing without forethought. Lots of forethought.

Kissing Kristen might have been the most impulsive thing he'd ever done, but it hadn't been thoughtless. He knew he'd never see her again. Even though they'd soon be in the same small country, there was a chasm of protocol between them. He'd deal with her boss because that was the level he was on. She'd deal with Stella because that was the level *she* was on. Nine chances out of ten he wouldn't even see her in passing.

He'd reasoned all that out before he'd kissed her and he'd been fine with it. But he hadn't counted on her lips being so soft or her kiss being so tempting. He hadn't counted on his head spinning and his hormones begging to take over. Still, he'd kept control. He'd stepped away like a gentleman.

And he'd eliminated a long plane ride with her by leaving for Grennady much later than his staff, and now here he was alone…

In the middle of the night.

In the frozen tundra.

Good God, it was cold!

And dark. Darker than he'd ever seen.

Of course, having grown up in the city, accustomed to streetlights, car lights and neon signs, he hadn't really been exposed to darkness.

He looked up and simply stared for a few seconds. The twinkle of a million stars, light-years away, almost stole his breath—which wouldn't be too hard to do since it was a visible puff of freezing air every time he exhaled.

Crap! It was cold!

And they'd lost a day. Considering time difference and travel across an ocean, it was late Monday night, early Tuesday morning, depending on how you looked at it. He was cold, late, and he'd had to force himself away from the first woman who'd really interested him in ten years. This trip was off to a fantastic start.

He wasted no time racing to the limo that awaited him. But instead of the driver opening the door, Kristen appeared at his side and pulled the latch to offer him entry.

"Good evening."

He had to shake himself to keep from staring at her. He'd meticulously planned it so he'd never see her again. Yet here she was.

He took another freezing breath to give himself time to recover from the shock, to stop the tingle that sprang to his lips, to fight his eyes from drinking in the sight of her. To get himself back into work mode. To remember she was an underling to the people with whom he'd be dealing for the next six weeks. And to speak normally.

"Evening? That's what you call this?"

"Actually, it's the dead of night. I went with *evening* because I thought *good night* would sound too much like goodbye—" She stopped abruptly and winced.

Internally, he winced too. They'd already had their goodbye in the form of a really great kiss. And just the thought of that kiss kicked his heart into high gear again.

Recovering quicker than he did, she smoothly motioned him inside the white limo. "We like to think of the darkness as cozy." She smiled. "Just wait until Christmas."

Her smile made him want to smile. But he refused. He had no intention of getting involved with this woman—for her sake, not his—and no intention of being a bundle of emotion around her. He would speak logic, behave logically and he would be fine.

When they were inside the limo, he pointed at her parka, thick mittens and the knit hat that hid her pretty yellow hair. "You can laugh because you're all bundled up."

"You'd think a genius would be smart enough

to realize he was traveling to one of the coldest countries in the world and dress appropriately."

He displayed the arm of his overcoat. "This is a winter coat."

She shook her head. "You're going to need something a little warmer."

"I'll call Stella."

Kristen put her hand on his wrist before he could pull out his phone. "She broke her leg."

Dean was so focused on how naturally, how easily she touched him, and how normal it felt to have her touch him, that he almost missed what she'd said. When it sunk in, he said. "Stella broke her leg?"

"Walking on the tarmac to get to the big jet, she lost her balance and fell. While we waited for the ambulance that took her to the ER, she insisted the flight go without her. When she's well enough to travel she said she'd catch up."

Dean sighed. "She needs to stay in bed for a few days, not fly across an ocean. I'll call her later and make sure she stays right where she is."

"Are you going to be okay without your right hand?"

"She's not my right hand. She's my people person."

"She talks to people for you?"

Dean peered at her, not sure if she was kidding. Jason had insisted he needed a date for the Christmas party to make him look normal, but they'd spent almost three entire days together. Surely, she didn't still think he was a social misfit. Though her having that wrong assumption might work to prevent her from getting the wrong idea about the kiss, it didn't sit well with his pride. He couldn't let her believe there was something hugely wrong with him.

"No. She takes care of things that involve other people. Like, when you needed a gown, she helped you get one. The employees needed to be rounded up and at the airport for their flight here, she arranged it."

He sighed, suddenly realizing the hole that would be left without Stella. "She was the one who would have been getting lift tickets and rental cars and all those things for the twenty people and their families we brought here."

He rubbed his hand across his mouth. "We're screwed."

"Your staff is smart enough to get their own lift tickets. And if they aren't, I have an entire palace staff at my disposal. With Eva and Alex in Xaviera for another two days, they're all yours. I'm happy to be your liaison."

His gaze crawled over to hers. So much for getting himself away from her. The royals were out of town, which he now remembered her telling him. Stella was out of commission. Until he got to know the palace staff, he needed her.

And he wasn't going to let his own personal longings get in the way. "Thank you. I appreciate the help."

"It's our pleasure. Even if Grennady only turns out to be a good place for your company to finish this one project, we want you to remember us fondly."

Right. His plan was exactly the opposite. She tempted him to want things he knew he couldn't have. So he intended to forget her, and everything about her.

"You want us to remember that your country didn't suit us so we left?"

"No. We want your employees to remember skiing and snowboarding. Sleigh rides. Hot cocoa. Hot toddies. Snuggling in front of fireplaces. We want them and their families to go home and talk about what a great time they had here."

He sniffed a laugh. "Leave it to you to find the bright side."

"Being in charge might be new to me, but I'm not stupid, and all of a sudden the timing feels right. Like I'm stepping into my destiny."

"Destiny." He snorted. He hated when people talked that way, as if some big hand would nudge them along, open doors, keep trouble at bay. She might be smart but that darned naïvety of hers was going to get her into trouble if she didn't put a lid on it. "Don't think destiny. Think to do list. Think organizational chart. For a charity like you're proposing, you'll need accountants and tax people, all of them versed in international law."

She laughed. "I haven't just kept a princess on track for three years, there's also the matter of that little degree you know I have. I'm more prepared for this than you think."

"You have a fanciful streak, as if you assume everything's going to automatically work out."

Her gaze ambled over and snagged his. "I got you here, didn't I?"

Desire slammed into him like a punch in the gut. She was tempting when she was sweet, but damned near irresistible when she was sassy.

He sucked in a breath and brought his briefcase to his lap so he wouldn't have to look at her when he spoke. "Technically, Mrs. Flannigan got me here."

"Yes, but it was a stroke of luck that I was with you every time you saw her."

"No, it wasn't luck. It was a bunch of things coming together. I took you to a Christmas party where Winslow invited us to lunch. You had told him you were pitching your country to me. He brought it up to Mrs. Flannigan. No magic. No destiny. More like logical steps. Everything had a purpose and a reason. Stop thinking about magic and destiny and start using this." He tapped her head. "And things will go a lot easier for you."

"I bet you're a real barrel of laughs at Christmastime."

He turned his attention to his briefcase, opening it as if he had something important he needed to read because once again he just couldn't look at her. "If I choose not to celebrate that particular holiday, I think I have good reason."

"Yes, you do. I'm sorry. I spoke thoughtlessly."

She looked so apologetic that he felt bad—for her. But he was the one who'd needed the reminder about mixing business with pleasure. If *he* wasn't so damned attracted to her, *he* wouldn't have fallen into such a complicated conversation. He would have told her what he needed. Told her yes or no. And the discussion would have stayed on track the way it should have.

"Look, it appears we're stuck working together for two days, so let's agree to stop trying to be friends and just do our jobs."

She gave him a funny look. "But you kissed me."

He sighed. Why was he not surprised her honesty wouldn't simply let that go?

"I know. I thought I was never going to see you again, so it wouldn't be a big deal. It was a nice way to end a nice weekend."

Her eyes softened when they met his. "A really nice weekend."

His pulse scrambled. It had been one of the nicest weekends of his life and to see she felt the same made him want to kiss her again. But he couldn't have her and she shouldn't want him.

"So let's leave it at that. A nice weekend." He rifled through the documents in his briefcase, pretending to be looking for something. "Right now my priority—and yours since you're my liaison—is to get this game to beta testers on January second. Forget about kisses, forget about the whole weekend. Hell, forget about Paris. Let's pretend we just met."

"Okay." She reached into her pocket. "You'll need this back, then."

The bracelet he'd given her fell into his briefcase. He'd told her he'd take it back, but actually having the damned thing almost fall into his lap sent a zap of weirdness through him. He'd bought that for her. He didn't want it back. It didn't feel right taking it back.

But if they were going to keep this strictly professional, he couldn't say any of that. He had to accept the bracelet.

"Great. Thanks. Are you sure you don't want it?"

"Totally."

He tucked it in his overcoat pocket and the weight of it felt like a rock. No one had ever returned a gift. He wasn't even sure what to do with it.

As they reached a hotel that looked more like a Swiss chalet, Kristen said, "The princess had to pull some strings, but we emptied the entire hotel and it's yours."

"Mine?"

"Well, yours and your employees'. You have the penthouse suite on the third floor. The first and second floors each have twenty rooms, so you've actually got an extra room or two. Just in case."

"So I'm in a hotel with my staff?"

"You'll be fine."

He shook his head. If Stella had booked this hotel, he would have accepted it on faith. Which was why they never fought or got personal. She did something. He accepted it.

So if he wanted to have an uncomplicated relationship with Kristen for the next two days, that's what he needed to do with her too. Not engage her. Just trust her judgment.

"Okay. Whatever. When do I see our work space?"

"Actually, your work space is the hotel's two first-floor meeting rooms."

He gaped at her. "We're working in the same space where we're living?"

"I thought you'd like that."

He blew his breath out on a sigh. Winslow had said to shake things up. So, sure. Why the hell not? "I might."

"It'll be very convenient. Staff has already been briefed on the fact that there's only about six hours of daylight. Most have decided to use the daylight for family time and work when it's dark."

This he could not handle. "I've gone along with

your conference rooms and having my employees and their families underfoot in my hotel... but eighteen hours of dark?"

She laughed. "It's winter in Scandinavia. Anybody who knows geography knows we don't get much daylight."

He struggled with the urge to close his eyes in frustration. He supposed he did know that. He simply hadn't put it all together.

"Look on the bright side. If your employees work when it's dark, that's eighteen whole hours a day."

He sniffed a laugh. "You are such a dreamer."

She climbed out of the limo. "Yeah, well, you're pretty much the opposite."

Of all the answers she could have given that was the last thing he'd been expecting. "That's it? I call you a dreamer and your best shot is to call me the opposite." He shook his head. "I'm absolutely going to have to teach you how to fight."

She smiled and pivoted toward the entryway. "Maybe I don't want to fight. Besides, that would take us back to you giving me lessons on how to handle myself in the business world. We just agreed to pretend we'd only met tonight. We can't go back to those lessons."

She walked into the hotel and he blew out another exasperated breath, staring at the starry sky.

Being with her, pretending he didn't like her, was going to kill him.

CHAPTER TEN

WHEN KRISTEN FINALLY got to bed, she slept like the dead. She woke around nine, just as the sun was coming up.

Curious about what she'd been doing the past few days, her family asked a million questions. She'd phoned them the day she'd flown to New York, in the limo on the way to the boutique to get her gown for the Christmas party with Dean, but they'd never heard of flying across an ocean with someone just to make a pitch. So she filled them in on the details of her trip and the weekend that followed, but her mom had trouble taking it all in.

"He's a busy man, Mom. People ask him to go places like lunches and dinners and I was his date for the weekend so I went too. But now we're in Grennady and everything's back to normal," she said as she grabbed a piece of cheese and headed for the door. "I can't do a darned thing to help him meet his deadlines, but I am in charge of making sure he and his crew are happy over the next two days. With his assistant in New York, I'm not sure what that's going to entail, but I need to be on-site."

She rushed out of her mom's kitchen and headed into town, to the men's shop where Prince Alex had bought his coat the first time he'd come to Grennady with Princess Eva, and realized he was horribly underdressed.

Stefan Steiner, a tall blond with big blue eyes, greeted her when she walked in. "Kristen! How can I help you?"

"The royal family has a visitor. An American."

"Oh, sounds interesting."

Dean was interesting, probably the most interesting guy Kristen had ever met. But he didn't want anything to do with her except a professional relationship, and she didn't want to push him into admitting he had feelings for her. Though he did. She knew he did. That kiss *told her* he did.

And she recognized that if he was avoiding

whatever was happening between them it was because he'd gotten his heart broken by Nina. She'd cheated him, used him, then dumped him.

And died.

Was it any wonder he was so careful about his feelings?

There was absolutely nothing Kristen could say or do without stepping on incredibly private territory, and if she pushed him he probably wouldn't talk anyway.

Realizing Stefan was waiting for an answer she said, "He's a businessman, only in Grennady for a few weeks trying to get some work done."

"Now? When we're about to celebrate Christmas?"

"He's American."

Stefan laughed. "Last time I heard, they celebrate Christmas in America."

She ambled toward a circle of parkas. "Not this guy. He's all about the work." Because his life had been difficult. Marred by tragedies that molded him into someone cool and precise with haunted eyes. But she couldn't dwell on that, couldn't wonder about the scar on his heart that might never really heal, or the days and nights of anguish he'd spent before he'd built his walls. Because when she let her mind go in that direction, she longed for him to talk to her, to get it out and see that he could be happy.

"So it's my job to make sure he doesn't have to worry about anything else." She picked a sturdy navy blue coat. "I think this is what he needs. I'm just not sure of the size."

Stefan joined her at the rack. "How tall is he?"

She glanced over. "About your height."

Stefan nodded. "Shoulder width?"

She frowned.

"How broad is he?"

"Well, he's…" She lifted her hands until she had them in a sort of circle the way they had been when she slid them to his nape when he kissed her. "This big."

Stefan eyed the shape made by her arms and told her the size Dean probably wore.

She shrugged. "Sounds good to me."

He helped her find warm gloves and a fur-lined bomber hat with flaps to cover his ears.

She nodded appreciatively. "He's probably

going to need boots too, but I won't even venture to guess that size."

"Yes, especially since you didn't kiss his feet."

Kristen felt her face color but she innocently said, "What?"

"You think I don't recognize the arm placement of someone kissing a man?"

She grimaced. "I guess you do."

He leaned across the counter. "Don't worry. My lips are sealed."

"Thanks. Because nothing's going to happen between us. Like I said. He's all about business." And no matter how haunted his eyes, she absolutely had to respect his wishes.

She signed off on the purchases, charging them to the royal family. Stefan told her to have Dean phone him with his boot size, and he'd have a pair delivered to his hotel.

She lugged the enormous bag out of his shop, passing familiar bakeries, groceries and restaurants on snow-covered streets that wafted with the scents of cheese, breakfast meats and breads. The frosty air nipped her nose and turned her breaths to puffs of smoke as she wove through gaggles of happy, chattering tourists.

In the lobby of the hotel the princess had procured for Dean and his staff, she stomped snow off her boots. After a quick chat with the desk clerk, she took her big package down the hall to the first meeting room.

Much larger than a conference room, more the size of a classroom, the space had round tables scattered throughout. Covered in white tablecloths as if prepared for a banquet, they weren't suitable for a bunch of computer geeks who would be working to find and fix the problems in software.

Given that it was light out and most of the Suminski Stuff staff were on the ski slopes with family, the hotel had plenty of time to put some workstations in there and maybe a sofa or recliner or two. She would remind them of that as soon as she gave Dean his coat, hat and gloves.

A few feet down the hall, she found the second meeting room. From the doorway, she could see this room was set up the same as the first.

Round tables with white tablecloths, each surrounded by six chairs.

The only difference was this room wasn't empty. Dean Suminski sat alone at one of the tables. Dressed in jeans and a sweater, with his hair causally mussed, he looked the way he had at Rockefeller Center. Memories of skating, holding hands, nestling against him as they walked up the busy New York City street slid through her brain, almost making her sigh with longing.

"In case you can't interpret the expression on my face, this empty room does not please me."

She laughed, though her heart jerked a bit. It was hard to believe that this guy currently being so cool with her had held her hand, built her confidence, introduced her to Mrs. Flannigan and made sure she had private time with her. And even harder to believe she had no choice but to go along with him.

"It's your employees' first day here. They may decide not to work at all today. I told you last night that they intended to take at least the daylight hours for family time. Your people need a break."

She hoisted the big bag containing his parka onto one of the round tables. "I bought you a few things."

One of his eyebrows quirked.

"Now you understand how I felt in New York when you kept buying me clothes."

"I told you that was the cost of doing business."

"Well, consider this a welcome gift from the royal family."

She pulled the hat out of the bag and tossed it to him, then the gloves, then the parka.

He caught the first two easily, but barely managed to grab the big coat. "I won't be going outside."

"You're here for six weeks. If nothing else, you'll tire of the hotel food and want to go to a restaurant. That coat you have won't cut it." She handed him Stefan's business card. "You'll also need boots. All you have to do is call Stefan and give him your size. He'll send the right boots to the hotel." She smiled hopefully. "Let's try everything on."

Hugging the big parka, Dean sighed in resignation and rose.

She took the coat from his hands and motioned for him to turn around. When he did, she held it open and guided the sleeves up his arms. After he shrugged into it, she smoothed her palms along the shoulders, straightening the fabric, recognizing it was a perfect fit.

But as her hands moved from his spine outward, she realized she was touching him. Essentially, rubbing his back. Because she liked it. She liked the feel of him, the look of him. Even the haunted expression in his eyes tempted her to ask him a million questions because she *wanted* to know him.

He turned his head and caught her gaze. "Having fun back there?"

She grimaced. "Sorry. I was just straightening things, making sure the coat fit."

"Right. And my lips accidentally bumped into yours when I kissed you."

His sarcastic wit would have surprised her, except he'd been making jokes all weekend, as he'd relaxed with her. She reached for the fur-lined navy blue hat with flaps that could be pulled down over his ears. Before he realized what she was about to do, she went to her tiptoes and plopped it on his head.

She burst into giggles. "You look like a Russian." But she quickly sobered. She really didn't know a damn thing about this guy she was so drawn to. "Are you Russian? With your dark hair and eyes, it wouldn't surprise me."

He gave the straps of the hat a tug to yank it into place. "I'm half Polish, half Irish."

"That's a strange combo."

He shrugged. "I'm sort of happy with it. The Polish part of me makes me resilient, and I've never met a Saint Patrick's Day that I didn't like."

The corners of her mouth tipped up into a smile. "There you are being funny again. You should let more people than me see your sense of humor."

"Oh, really? And what do you think Winslow

would have done Friday night if I'd cracked jokes when my company was in trouble?"

"Maybe thought you were human?"

"Or thought I wasn't serious. Or thought I didn't realize how much trouble I was in."

"Well, I don't care." She reached up and linked the two straps of the hat under his chin, securing them in their catch. "I like it when you're funny."

He caught her hand to stop it. "You shouldn't."

Once again they were standing incredibly close, almost as if they couldn't help themselves. "Why are you so determined to ignore what we feel for each other?"

"Because I'm not anybody's knight in shining armor, Kristen."

"Only because you were hurt."

"And that turned me into the kind of guy who isn't made for relationships."

He didn't have the look of longing that usually came to his eyes when they stood this close. For a few seconds, she missed it, and then she understood what he was saying. Away from the trouble that threw them together in the first place, he was in control again.

And maybe he didn't like her as much as she'd thought.

She cleared her throat. "Now that you have a coat, you should go out. Go find your people on the ski slopes. Have some fun."

"Yeah, Dean, maybe you should."

Kristen whipped around to see Dean's right-hand man, Jason, standing in the doorway. Dressed in a colorful sweater that made his twenty or so extra pounds all the more obvious, he sauntered into the room, holding a cup of coffee.

Dropping her hand, Dean said, "What are you doing here?"

"Stella's down for the count." He shrugged. "She's got a few days of really good drugs for the pain and then six weeks in some sort of boot thing, then a few weeks of rehab."

Dean winced. "Ouch."

"Yeah, she says 'ouch' a lot." He laughed. "Anyway, I thought you might need me. So I flew over."

"Thank God." Dean breathed an insulting sigh of relief, as if Kristen didn't cut it as his assistant. "I do need you. *This* is where the royal family decided we should work."

Jason didn't answer. He glanced at Kristen.

Kristen held her breath. One wrong word from Jason and she'd be looking for another place for them, and she didn't have the clout of a princess.

Jason glanced around, took a sip of coffee and said, "I like it."

Dean scowled.

Kristen's heart about exploded with relief.

"Winslow Osmond said the staff needed a change of scenery, but I was thinking maybe we need a change in the way we're doing things too," Jason said. "What can it hurt to have all the key players in the same room?"

"They could kill each other."

Jason shrugged off his boss's concern. "Or they could learn to work together." He ambled over to Dean. He pinched a bit of the sleeve of the parka. "What's this?"

"A coat, gloves and some hat thing," Dean said, peering at Kristen as if the coat and hat had somehow ruined his life.

Jason nodded. "I like them." He caught Dean's gaze. "So technically you *could* go skiing."

Dean just looked at him.

Jason faced Kristen. "Truth be told, he's not a skier. But he used to be hell with a snowboard."

"*Used to* being the operative words," Dean said.

But Kristen pictured a much younger Dean, in a cooler coat and a trendy knit cap. Having seen him laugh, she guessed he'd probably laughed on the slopes, that he'd loved the challenge of the snowboard and the rush of speed as he flew down winding hills. Once again her heart ached that one tragic episode in his life had taken a probably happy young man and turned him into someone afraid to live.

Jason smiled. "You know what? You might not want to jump on a snowboard today, but you should get out and see the town." He turned to Kristen. "Your capital is amazing."

Kristen said, "Thank you. Most of the buildings have been around for centuries."

Jason nodded. "You don't see craftsmanship like that anymore." He pivoted to face Dean.

"You need to go out and see some of this." Then back to Kristen. "Kristen, would you take him?"

Kristen said, "I can't," at the same time that Dean said, "We have work to do."

Jason waved both hands. "Oh, garbage, you two. You'll work tonight. Or tomorrow when our wayward staff is scheduled to be here. Go now, while you still have—" He glanced at his watch. "What? Four hours of sunlight?"

"That's about it," Kristen agreed.

"Good." He faced Dean. "It's not so long that you'll get bored. But it's enough time to see some of the sights. And clear your head. Get some fresh air into those lungs."

Dean's scowl grew.

Jason faced Kristen. "Whether he understands it or not, he's going to want to compliment your king and princess when they return from their holiday in Xaviera. Give him a little bit of a history lesson so he can speak intelligently."

"No. I'm not going anywhere."

CHAPTER ELEVEN

DEAN'S REFUSAL RANG through the quiet work space. Jason took a step back, as if he knew he'd pushed too far.

But Kristen sucked in a hard breath. Dean had hurt her, and he'd done it deliberately, but he decided that's what she needed to see. The demanding, difficult side of him that everybody thought was the real him.

She turned and headed for the door. "If you need anything I'll be in the palace."

He didn't say goodbye. He didn't say anything. He waited for her to leave, and then he faced Jason. "Get maintenance back here. I want this room and the one up the hall ready for work when that blasted sun goes down."

With that he exited, heading up the hall to the elevator that would take him to his pent-house suite. When the door opened on the modern space with red sofas and black and white accent pieces, he wrestled out of the big coat he didn't want and threw the damned hat at the cold fireplace.

He wasn't just angry that Kristen kept pushing him to be the person he was deep down inside. He was angry that he couldn't be that guy.

He got on the phone and made some calls and forgot all about Kristen Anderson. But when the sun went down and his employees began returning, laughing, happy, more enthusiastic than he'd seen them in weeks, guilt set in. When an hour went by with everybody getting along, making accommodations for each other in the unusual work space and sharing ideas for what they should do next with the games, the guilt tripled.

Winslow and Mrs. Flannigan had been right. They needed this time somewhere different, somewhere they could relax, somewhere their creativity could be nurtured. Kristen had found him, essentially had made this four-week getaway possible, and he'd thanked her by treating her like dirt.

* * *

After dinner with her family, Kristen went upstairs and opened her laptop. Mrs. Flannigan had given her a list of people to consider for her board of advisors but before she approached anyone she wanted to know a bit about them.

But reading resumes for and articles about people who were wealthy because they were brilliant, only reminded her of Dean. How she'd wanted him to be the playful guy she'd uncovered in New York and how he'd bitten her head off. It hadn't taken a real yelling session. She'd gotten the message from the way he'd said no to a tour with her.

It had stung, though. Because deep down she believed he liked her. And it stung even more, because deep down she had more feelings for him than she'd let herself admit.

The sound of sleigh bells penetrated the haze of her thoughts, then two male voices, and she frowned. Her family's farm was far enough off the beaten path that no one "accidentally" drove or walked by. She rose from her desk and looked out the window.

At the edge of the road was a pretty red sleigh decorated with yellow flowers and green leaves. The driver sat on the bench seat, holding the reins of a chestnut mare. Dean Suminski sat in the backseat.

She spun around and raced out of her room and down the stairs to the front door, so thrilled to see him that she didn't care why he'd chosen a sled to come to her house. She hadn't been wrong about his feelings for her, and that, once again, quadrupled her feelings for him.

With a laugh, she whipped open the door. "What are you doing?"

Walking up to the porch of her parents' house, he wore the big blue parka and the hat, with the flaps over his ears. He angled his thumb toward the sleigh. "This is an apology."

Her heart stumbled. The great Dean Suminski apologized? "For what?"

"I was a bit nastier in my refusal of a tour of your capital than I wanted to be."

Her heart stuttered. "A bit nastier? Did you intend to be nasty?"

He sighed. "No. I just felt overwhelmed."

She could have said, "Overwhelmed by what?" and forced the issue that he was having trouble with the fact that he wanted to be himself around her. Except he was here. Outside the door of her parents' house...with a sleigh! He *wanted* to see her. He didn't need to say the words. And she didn't need to push for them.

"So is everything going okay at the hotel?"

"Yes." He nodded at her white sweater and jeans. "You're freezing without a coat. Go get one. We'll talk while we ride."

He turned and began walking back to the sleigh. She spun around, raced into her house and grabbed her coat, hat and mittens.

Her mother, a tall, thin blonde wearing a colorful apron over jeans, walked into the front hall. "Kristen? Did I hear you talking to someone?"

"Dean Suminski, the guy I went to New York with...he's here with a sleigh."

Her mom frowned. "The man working at the hotel?"

Sliding into her coat, she nodded.

Her mom said, "You should invite him to dinner."

Kristen froze. Invite him to dinner? Have him meet her parents? That would probably freak him out. "Didn't we already eat?"

"I didn't mean tonight. I meant tomorrow or Friday," her mom said with a laugh. Then she shooed her out the door. "Go. Have fun."

Kristen raced out onto the big front porch of her family's old farmhouse and down the three steps to the snow-covered sidewalk. Dean stood by the sleigh. When she reached him, he helped her climb inside, then pulled himself in behind her.

The air was crisp, the night freezing cold, but, God help her, to her it felt just plain magical. Every step he took was a step closer to him being the man he was supposed to be, the man who could love her.

She slowed her thoughts. Told her brain to settle down. He was a broken man. A man who'd grown up without love, whose first love had used him. She wasn't going to wave a magic wand and he'd be normal again. His wounds might be healing, but he would need time to learn to trust again.

Still, she knew her heart was racing ahead of things because she had feelings for him far beyond anything she'd ever felt. If she wanted this, wanted him, and she did, she had to take her time. Give him a way to get to know her enough that he'd trust her with his heart. Not rush. Not nudge. Just enjoy the sleigh ride.

After all…he was here, wasn't he?

Spreading a thick blanket over both of their legs, he said, "I actually learned how to drive the sleigh from the internet. YouTube."

She glanced over, saw he was serious and laughed. "So why aren't you driving?"

"Clyde up there," he said, pointing to their driver, "knows his way around the countryside. I don't."

"Good point."

Powdery snow muffled the clip-clop of the horse's hooves, but caused the sleigh blades to make a *swoosh, swoosh, swoosh* noise as the sled moved along. A light in the front illuminated twenty or so feet ahead, but otherwise her world, her county, was dark and silent.

Dark, *freezing cold* and silent.

The kind of cold where two people who shouldn't like each other, shouldn't belong together, could snuggle under a cover and get to know each other.

She slid her arm beneath his, nestled close, seeking his warmth but also basking in the chance to touch him.

"So tell me more about what you did today."

"Being this far away from the US and being plunged into darkness more hours of the day than any human being should have to endure has had an odd effect on me."

She cuddled closer. "Let's not forget that it's cold."

He stiffened, but he said, "It is cold." Then he slowly relaxed beside her, as if he couldn't deny he wanted the closeness too, and using the cold as an excuse made that easier. "But it seems to work. The employees came back today more energetic than I've seen them in months."

He leaned back, relaxed. Saying all that out loud seemed to have helped it to sink in that everything was working out.

"I'm glad we could help."

"It's just…" He turned to look at her. "Unexpected."

She couldn't have said it any better herself. What was happening between them was unexpected. But maybe that was part of the attraction. She was an unsophisticated country girl. He was a guy who had pulled himself up by his talent and his genius and made himself one of the most important men in the business world. But they clicked.

They rode through the silent night for about twenty minutes with her prodding him with questions, getting him to talk about his work.

"Jason thinks I should stop the US calls when the team comes in off the slopes. And forget about Asia until we get home. He says the team wasn't just energetic because they'd had fun on the ski slopes. He thinks they respond positively to having me around." He stole a peek at her. "Normally, I'm in my office four floors above them and they work on their own. Today, I spent time in the meeting room, asking questions, giving suggestions." He shrugged. "It was fun. Like the old days."

"Maybe you *should* spend more time with them."

"I haven't touched that part of the company in years."

"That's interesting since they've been stuck for years."

He shook his head. "If you're hinting that they need me, don't. I've hired the best in the business. They don't need me."

"And yet…here they are…stuck."

He sniffed a laugh and she let the subject die, knowing she'd gotten her point across.

As the night got colder, their blanket drifted higher, to their chins. She reveled in the way he talked, the sound of his voice, the quiet trust. The sleigh turned around, headed back, and she knew she had only another twenty minutes.

When he asked how her day had been, she returned the favor of being honest with him the way he'd been with her. "When the princess is away I'm bored. I have nothing to do but check her email a few times a day to make sure nothing that comes in is a crisis." She peeked at him.

"And as small as we are, we get a crisis about once every ten years."

He laughed. "Too bad you can't code."

"Really?" She knew he hadn't intended to take them down this road, but this was the heart of why she always wanted to be around him and why he'd brought a sleigh to her house in the dead of night. And maybe it was time they talked about it.

"You think it's a bad thing that we're different?"

He faced her, held her gaze for a few seconds.

When she couldn't take the honest scrutiny anymore, she whispered, "Admit it. Part of the attraction is that we're nothing alike."

He looked around her frozen countryside. "We might have been raised differently and have two different ways in which we want to change the world." He met her gaze again. "But we both want to change the world."

"So? That just means we're enough alike that we understand each other, but different enough that we're interesting."

He shook his head. The sleigh silently swooshed to a stop in front of her parents' farmhouse.

"Maybe. I don't know."

He appeared genuinely perplexed. She supposed if someone tossed a monkey wrench into her life she'd be confused too. But even with the totally baffled expression on his face, he was handsome, strong. She couldn't resist leaning forward and touching her lips to his. She stayed there a second, giving him time to respond and he did. Under their blanket, his hands came up to her shoulders to pull her close so he could deepen the kiss.

And she realized this was what she'd been waiting for her whole life. The magic prince she didn't believe existed wasn't a guy on a white horse; he was someone who understood her. Someone she understood. An equal.

She broke the kiss and slid out from under the cover, bolting out of the sleigh before he had a chance to get out into the cold when he didn't have to.

They were falling in love. Real love.

She turned and waved. "I'll see you tomorrow."

Then she pivoted around and ran into her house. Her blood racing. Her knees a little weak. But her heart happy as well as terrified.

They clicked. That's why everything felt so different when they were together.

But she had only four weeks to get him to see it.

And even if he did, he'd have to brave a whole new world of communication and honesty. He might not be capable of having the kind of relationship she needed.

CHAPTER TWELVE

THE NEXT DAY Dean woke feeling happy, refreshed. Jason joined him in the penthouse suite for breakfast.

After room service wheeled in their cart, Jason said, "So where'd you go last night?"

Dean kept his attention on his tablet. He'd pulled up *the Wall Street Journal* and was reading the highlights of the day's financial news.

After he finished the article, he glanced up at his friend. "Believe it or not, I hired a sleigh."

Jason laughed. "Sleigh?"

"I figured I owed Kristen an apology for barking at her yesterday when she was trying to be helpful." He shook his head in wonder. "I never knew darkness could be so appealing."

"You've lived too long in the city," Jason said, lifting the lid off his plate of eggs and pancakes.

"When we get back home, we'll start scheduling more time for you in your Albany house."

Just the thought of the Albany house made him smile. He knew it was because of the vision he'd had of Kristen in that house, on his bed, with his child. Though the vision didn't scare him to death or confuse him as it had the first time he thought it, it did fill him with questions.

Was that what he was doing with her? Falling in love so he could have something he wasn't even sure existed? The sleigh ride hadn't been as romantic as it had been warm, nice. Then she'd kissed him and, of course, everything that had been warm and friendly suddenly became hot and steamy.

He'd thought of her the whole way back to town, thought of her when he woke up and now he was thinking of her again.

He just liked her. Everything about her.

Even her freezing cold country.

And it scared him to death.

He'd liked everything about Nina too. Even her sweltering hot country. When it came to falling in love, he had no guidelines, no common sense.

He'd been gobsmacked when Nina told him she'd been using him to make Alex Sancho jealous.

So what would he find out about Kristen? That she had used him to get to know Mrs. Flannigan? That being connected to him gave her a stature that would help her establish herself in his world and easily get the money she needed for her charity?

Because there was something.

There was always something.

A few minutes later, the suite phone rang. Not knowing who would have the number, he didn't answer. Embroiled in a discussion of marketing techniques in Asia, Jason didn't even acknowledge that the phone had rung.

But after Jason left to go do some sightseeing, Dean checked with the front desk. They had indeed taken a message from the call he'd ignored.

"Kristen Anderson called. She'd like you to join her family this evening for dinner. Seven o'clock. She left a number."

Dean said, "Thank you. I won't need the number." Because he did not intend to go to that family dinner.

But all day long he thought of the white farmhouse he'd glimpsed when his sleigh had swished up to her sidewalk. He thought about the fact that it was so far out in the country and wondered about the people who lived there...

And the people who had raised Kristen. What kind of parents were so strong that they raised a daughter who took up the cause of a pen pal who'd been killed? What kind of parents raised a child to be so open and honest? Did she have brothers and sisters?

In the end, he waited until the very last second, until it was too late to call and say he was coming. So late, he barely got a cab.

He arrived at her house, bottle of wine in hand—the suggestion of the cabbie—and knocked on the door, wondering what in the hell he was doing.

The door opened. A tall, blonde woman smiled broadly at him. "You must be Dean Suminski." She opened the door a little wider. "I'm Joan, Kristen's mom." She motioned for him to enter, then turned and called up the stairs, "Kristen! Your friend is here."

As Dean stepped inside the old-fashioned foyer, Joan faced him with a smile. "I hope you like roast beef. We're not fancy here."

Feeling odd and awkward, he said, "That's great," just as Kristen came running down the stairs. She stopped when she saw him and their gazes met.

She wore jeans and a white sweatshirt. Her hair fell around her in loose curls. But her smile was huge, luscious. As if seeing him made her the happiest woman in the world.

Now, how the hell was he supposed to resist that?

"I'm so glad you came."

"Yeah, well, I'm sorry I didn't call."

"There was no reason to call," Kristen's mom said, taking his arm and guiding him through the short hall that led to an unexpectedly modern kitchen. "We don't stand on ceremony here."

He walked up to the center island that was cluttered with pots and pans, utensils and dishes used to make the dinner. The hardwood floors sparkled. The other counters were neat and tidy. A table in the adjoining dining area had been set.

Kristen said, "I'll set another place."

As she scrambled to gather plates, Kristen's mom nodded at a stool by the center island and he sat.

"Kristen's dad should be in any minute," Joan said, rifling through a drawer. She pulled out a corkscrew and handed it to him with the wine he'd brought. "You do the honors." She turned to the dining area. "Kristen, would you also get wineglasses?"

He opened the wine as Kristen retrieved wine-glasses from a cabinet with a glass front. She set the four glasses on the counter, then smiled at him.

Warmth invaded his heart. Warmth and ease and a kind of comfort he'd never felt before.

The back door opened and an older man entered, a teenage boy on his heels.

"This is Kristen's dad, James, and her youngest brother, Lars. Lars, Jimmy, this is Kristen's friend Dean. He's the man who brought his company here for a bit of a rest while they work."

He didn't question that they knew about him. He would expect Kristen to tell her family about her work. Given the relaxed atmosphere of the kitchen, he would expect that she talked about everything in her life with her parents, and that they talked freely with her.

"It's a pleasure to meet you."

The big man walked over and clasped his hand. "It's a pleasure to meet you, too. Kristen's been all about trying to get a company here to Grennady, especially since her other brother, Brian, is studying computer science at university."

Dean peeked over at Kristen who blushed. "She never mentioned that."

Her gaze met his. "I didn't want to unduly influence you."

That made him laugh. Really laugh. The kind of laugh he experienced with her in New York. "Are you kidding? You stalked me to Paris, wouldn't get off my plane in New York until I listened to your pitch. And now you're trying to say you didn't want to influence me?"

She winced. "All right. Maybe a little."

Kristen's father and brother went upstairs to wash up for dinner. Dean poured the wine. He sat at the center island while Kristen cleared the counter and her mom put the finishing touches on dinner. By the time the men returned, dinner was ready to serve.

They spent the meal discussing Dean's company, Kristen's charity and the possibility that Lars would be going into computer science too. They sat around the table, eating chocolate cake for dessert, finishing the wine, talking like old friends, not worrying about clearing dishes. Until at nine o'clock when Kristen volunteered to drive him home.

He realized that her parents probably had to get up early the next morning and took his jacket when Joan brought it from the newel post on the stairway in the foyer.

"I can get a cab."

Shrugging into her coat, Kristen said, "Nonsense. It's not that far."

Then she smiled that smile again, the one that made him feel warm all over, the one that made him feel very much a part of her life, and the one he couldn't resist.

They got into her little car and he let her have

her concentration to maneuver out of the farm's lane and onto the snow-covered main road.

"Your family is really nice."

"Yes. They are. We're just average, normal people, living life." She peeked at him. "I appreciate you being so nice to them. My mom really wanted to meet you. She was thrilled you accepted her dinner invitation."

"She's a great cook."

"Hey, I made those potatoes."

"Then you're probably a good cook too." He took a breath, considered for only a few seconds, then said, "My Gram had been a really great cook in her time, but the older she got the less she wanted to cook." He shrugged. "We ate a lot of pizza."

"As a little kid you probably liked that."

He laughed. "I did."

"Other stuff, not so much."

"I just always felt left out. She wouldn't let me sign up for Little League, or even after school activities. Said we couldn't afford the fees and insisted there always were fees. If there were parent-teacher conferences, I knew she wouldn't go. It's why it took so long for anyone to recognize that I was gifted."

"It sounds like she was just overwhelmed."

"She was."

"It also sounds like you forgive her."

"In a weird kind of way, there was nothing to forgive her for. Even as a kid I recognized that I was a burden."

"That's not a very nice way for a kid to feel."

He shook his head. "No."

"But you're over it."

"Most of it." He shrugged. "Lots of it. But there are some things you can't get over. All you can do is adjust."

"Nothing wrong with that."

No. He supposed there wasn't. He also couldn't believe how free he felt talking about this with her.

When she pulled the car into a parking space in front of the hotel, he glanced around, confused. He'd thought she'd drop him off at the door. Instead, they were in the back.

He turned to ask her why they were parked, just as she stretched across the seat and kissed him. Quick and light, her lips brushed his, and then she pulled back again.

"Thanks for coming tonight."

He laughed. "You're welcome. That's the first time anybody's ever kissed me as a thank-you."

Her head tilted. "Really?" She leaned forward and kissed him again. "Now you've been kissed twice as a thank-you."

This time he didn't let her pull back, he caught her shoulders and kept her right where she was so he could deepen the kiss. He had absolutely no idea what was happening, but if this was love, he really liked it.

After a few minutes, he realized he was necking in a car—in a hotel parking lot, with a woman he really liked who was nothing like any other woman he'd ever gotten involved with—like a horny teenager.

He took her shoulders and set her away from him, back on the driver's side of the car.

"That was different."

She laughed. "Really?"

"All this is so normal for you. So easy—"

"You think? You think I just go around kissing

random guys?" She laughed gaily. "It's every bit as unusual for me as it is for you. And maybe even really poor timing for me since I'm at the beginning of the project I hope will be my life's work."

He sobered. "I'm sorry."

She laughed again, then shook her head. "Seriously, you need to work on thinking before you talk. I'm not saying this is a bad thing. It's a good thing. What I'm saying is that what we feel comes with complications." She stretched around again so that she could look into his eyes. "My family's putting up our Christmas tree on Saturday afternoon. I'd love for you to come."

Sitting so close, staring into her eyes, all he could think to say was, "Yes."

She pulled back. "Take the next few days to think things through." She put the car into gear again and drove up to the hotel door. "I'll see you Saturday."

Dazed, confused, he said, "Okay," as he got out of the car. But he understood what she was saying. The timing was wrong for them. Plus, he had issues. He might not be tumbling head-first into love as much as he could be tumbling headfirst into disaster.

Saturday afternoon, Kristen was surprised when the doorbell rang and Dean stood on the front porch of her home, holding two bottles of wine.

Her heart spun crazily. She absolutely hadn't expected him to come to her house again. She believed he'd talk himself out of it. First, though he'd been comfortable with her family, she could see him returning to his hotel, picking the evening apart and finding a million things wrong with him getting to know her parents and brother. Second, she was positive he'd decide his work was more important than an afternoon off. Third, they were going to decorate a tree and Christmas was not his favorite holiday. Fourth, she was very sure what he felt for her confused him.

But confused or not, he was on her porch.

"Come in."

He stepped into the foyer, handed her the wine

and shrugged out of his jacket, which he casually hung across the newel post again.

"You brought extra wine to help you get through this, didn't you?"

He laughed and brushed a quick kiss across her mouth. "Sort of."

Though his answer didn't surprise her, the quick kiss did. She couldn't imagine what he felt for her, that the man who didn't even like talking to people was willing to take himself this far out of his comfort zone for her.

She led him into the kitchen, where they grabbed four wineglasses, then into the living room where a huge blue spruce sat in the corner.

Dean said hello to her family, then uncorked the wine and poured, not really looking at the tree or the decorations that were strewn all over the chairs, sofa and coffee table.

She picked up an ancient ornament and presented it to him. "I made this in kindergarten."

His eyes narrowed. "Is that a—?"

"Toilet paper roll? Yes. Covered in glitter and tinsel, but it's still a toilet paper roll."

He laughed.

Lars picked up his corresponding roll. "Mine."

Dean laughed again. "It's nice that you saved them."

Kristen's mom said, "We like to remember Christmases past."

Kristen's gaze flew to Dean. But he hardly responded. If she hadn't known to look for the quiet indrawn breath, she wouldn't even have known the comment had affected him.

Still, she'd seen the breath. But though she knew walking through a family's Christmas memories might be difficult for him, she also knew he needed to do this. He needed to stop avoiding the holiday that gave most people pure joy and get involved, so that someday he'd feel a part of that joy.

"Grandma Anderson lived with us till her passing when I was in high school. She loved to make nut rolls."

As her father reached to loop a string of lights over the tree, he said, "There was nothing like warm nut roll on Christmas morning."

"With a glass of milk," Lars agreed.

Dean set down his wine and walked over to

the tree. Standing on the opposite side of her father, he caught the strings of lights when her dad tossed them, placed them on a branch—as her father had been doing—and guided them back to her dad.

Knowing there was no time like the present, Kristen said, "So do you have any special memories, Dean?"

Kristen's mother's eyes widened and her dad's head jerked toward Kristen, but she knew this was what had to be done. Face the elephant in the room head-on.

Dean quietly said, "No." Working with the lights, he kept his gaze averted. Still, Kristen knew this was the best thing for him, so she persisted.

"I told my parents about your parents."

Apparently finally figuring out what Kristen was doing, her mom jumped in saying, "That was tragic and difficult for you."

"Yes. It was," Dean said.

"Worse that your grandmother was too old to care for you," Joan said sympathetically.

With all that out in the open, Kristen knew it

was time to shift gears. "But that's over now. And you have an entire holiday of traditions to investigate and experiment with. Lars, why don't you get a tray of those fruit horns Mom made this morning?"

Not needing to be asked twice, Lars raced out of the room.

Dean looked up at her mother, his head tilting as he studied her. "These cookies are good?"

"These cookies are excellent," Kristen's mom answered without a hint of humility. "Christmas baking is my specialty. If you like banana nut bread, you'll be thrilled when you eat mine."

Dean laughed. "Okay. Bring on the cookies."

Kristen breathed a sigh of relief. With Dean's past now acknowledged, Dean didn't have to pretend anymore. Kristen would have been thrilled that her idea had worked out, except in New York, she'd seen Dean noticing Christmas decorations, being part of Christmas celebrations.

He had been ready to not just acknowledge there was a Christmas, but also to ease himself into it.

But she was falling in love with him—and he'd

been hurt, used in the worst possible way. A few Christmas cookies and an afternoon decorating a tree wouldn't be enough to get him past Nina.

He might never get past Nina.

And then what would she do? Be in love with a man who couldn't trust enough to return her feelings?

CHAPTER THIRTEEN

ON MONDAY MORNING, the royals had been back for three days and were settled in. Rumor around the palace was that Dean had been invited to dinner Sunday night, and that he and Alex had been cordial. No one expected them to become best friends, but for Grennady's sake, Kristen was glad they'd made a peace of a sort.

Around noon, Kristen's intercom buzzed. She pressed the button. "Yes?"

Eva said, "Kristen, could I see you in my office, please."

"Of course."

When she walked into Eva's office, Prince Alex rose from his chair beside Eva's. He smiled. "Sit."

Confusion rumbled through her, but she sat.

Eva said, "We understand you and Dean spent time together while we were away."

"Yes. I mentioned to you already that he needed a guest for a Christmas party and when he brought his staff here I kept our relationship going to make sure he and his staff were comfortable."

"He told us that he's advising you on your charity, specifically talking about your board of advisors."

"He told you that?"

"Yes. We had a very good conversation." Eva reached out and took Alex's hand. "This isn't an easy situation for any of us. But ten years have gone by, and Xaviera's Royal Guard, headed by Alex's brother, absolved Dean of any guilt in the death of their mutual friend. It was time to let go."

Kristen sat back on her seat. She tried to picture Dean's reaction to that and couldn't. The royals might not blame him for Nina's death, but Nina had used him.

"Which was how the conversation naturally flowed to you and your charity. Dean is very impressed. We've always been impressed with you. And now that everything seems to be falling into place, Alex and I would like to offer our suggestions on that too."

"I'd love to hear them."

"We also want to be one of your first benefactors. As soon as you have your corporation and bank accounts set up, we'll be donating a million dollars."

Kristen's face fell. "Thank you."

Alex said, "We also think it's time for you to quit your post here."

Something inside of Kristen blossomed to life. For years she'd been dreaming, researching, and the day was finally here. She was going to do something important not for herself but for the world.

The thrill of it shimmied through her and she sat up taller in her chair. "Yes. It is. Thank you."

"So as of today, you're free." Eva laughed. "Which means I now have to give you a formal invitation to the reception we'll be hosting tonight for Suminski Stuff. Because you were the one who got them here, we'll feel it's only right you attend the reception—as yourself, not an employee anymore."

Kristen rose. "Thank you, ma'am."

Eva rose too. "Sweetie, you can call me Eva now. After all, if I'm on your board of advisors, I'll sort of be working for you."

The reception that night hosted by King Mason to honor the guests from Suminski Stuff was as formal as a ball, just a lot smaller. Kristen dressed in a pink lace gown she'd bought for the royal Christmas Eve party the year before. She wasn't one to care about wearing the same dress twice. She'd actually seen Princess Eva do it. Plus, now that she was officially on her own, every cent she spent had meaning.

The princess straightened the cap sleeves of her gown. "You look perfect. Very smart. Are you ready for this?"

Kristen laughed. "I think dealing with Dean prepared me for a lot of it."

Eva said, "Hmm… I hope you're being careful with him. His upbringing made him ruthless. That's not something a man gets over or forgets. It's part of who he is."

"I'm fine with him. In fact, I like him."

"Like him?"

With everything happening so fast in her life, Kristen decided it was time to take another plunge. "He's very different with me than he is with other people. He's been to dinner at my house, helped my family decorate our tree."

"Oh, my gosh." Eva's eyes widened. "You're in love with him."

Kristen winced. "I think. Yes."

Eva shook her head. "Just be careful."

Eva's gown swished as she led Kristen from the staging area to the receiving line for the reception. Eva's father, King Mason, a tall, fair man stood with her mother, Queen Karen, who wore a black velvet gown and a diamond necklace—her gift from her husband for being so understanding about why he'd left her out of the details of their near coup the winter before.

The king saw Kristen and Eva entering, and a smile blossomed on his face. He took both of Kristen's hands. "I understand congratulations are in order."

She bowed. "Thank you, Your Majesty."

"The queen and I would also like to add a donation to your school project."

Humbled, she bowed again. "Thank you, very much."

Queen Karen hugged her. "Don't thank us. You're the star. Mr. Suminski using our country— even if it's only for short-term projects—is huge for us." She smiled. "And we have you to thank for that."

Kristen laughed. "I just took things one step at a time."

King Mason said, "Then that's what you keep doing."

They entered the reception room and took their places in the receiving line. Two butlers opened the wide double doors, offering entry to Dean first, who bowed to the king and queen, shook hands with Alex and Eva, and took a place next to King Mason, as the evening's official guest of honor.

Then the doors were opened and Dean's employees entered. Wide-eyed with amazement and curiosity, they glanced around the ornate reception room. Other dignitaries and guests filtered in, including the ones Princess Eva wanted Kristen to meet.

As Dean shook hands and talked of software and stock prices, Kristen spoke to the same guests, making plans to meet potential advisors and benefactors for lunch or dinner.

In what felt like a flick of a switch, her entire life changed.

Because Dean was with the king and queen, and Kristen was with the princess and Alex, their paths didn't cross until after dinner when the king and his wife mingled and Eva and Alex danced.

Kristen saw Dean standing off to the side with Jason and she walked over.

"Hello, again."

Jason all but bowed. "Hello, again, to you too. It's quite a night for you."

She laughed. "I've been building to this for years. I wasn't always giving a big push for my schools, but raising money and looking for people to help find real estate, teachers, textbooks was always in the back of my mind." She took a long satisfied breath. "Now it's a reality." She turned to Dean. "Would you like to dance?"

Jason laughed. "Look at her. Her first official event as a leader and she's already bold enough to ask a guy to dance." He turned to Dean. "This is going to sound so odd, but you know who she reminds me of? Nina. Now there was a woman who was bold."

His comment seemed out of place to Kristen, but she knew Jason and Dean had history. What he'd said probably made sense to Dean. Even if Kristen had no clue what he meant.

Dean put his drink on the tray of a passing waiter. In her pink dress, with her hair piled high on her head, Kristen looked as regal, as elegant as Princess Eva.

But she was more than royalty. She was an honest, open, wonderful person. Someone who liked him. Someone he liked—and trusted. She was nothing like Nina.

He smiled. "I'd love to dance."

They walked out onto the dance floor and he smoothly took Kristen into his arms. As always, she felt like an equal. In a weird kind of way, she'd always been his equal.

No, if he remembered correctly, the night of their first Christmas party, in New York, he'd realized she was the woman of his dreams. The woman who could be his partner. Smart and sassy enough to keep him on his toes and beautiful enough to hold him spellbound, Kristen Anderson was everything he wanted.

And this was his moment.

"So how was your day?"

He laughed because her question, everything about the night felt right. Actually, a part of him was a little giddy.

"I snowboarded."

Her eyes widened. "On your own?"

"Yes." He smiled. "I took one of the buses that runs to the slopes and rented a board."

A laugh bubbled up. "No kidding."

"On the slopes I had some interesting revelations."

"Sounds serious."

He spun her around to change that mood. What he felt for her was serious, but it was also fun.

Spontaneous. Wonderful. Snowboarding for the first time in a decade, he realized he'd already pushed through the hard stuff. Meeting her parents. Talking about his situation in front of them. Decorating a tree with her family. Eating cookies. And he knew that with everything in their relationship moving at the speed of light, he shouldn't stop what was happening between them. He should grab this opportunity and run with it.

But he wouldn't tarnish that by being ominous. He liked wonderful. He could get addicted to wonderful.

"My revelation wasn't serious as much as it was true. Coming to terms with everything with Prince Alex at dinner last night, I felt like I was knocked back to the place I was ten years ago."

She frowned. "Ten years ago? When you were starting out?"

Her question reminded him of Jason's comment that she reminded him of Nina. It was ridiculous. She was nothing like Nina. "When I met the Saudi prince I wasn't so much starting out as I was collecting capital. I knew I was good at what I did. I was also learning to have fun." His eyes met hers. She might be "nothing" like Nina, but they did have the common denominator that they'd both pushed him out of his comfort zone to have fun. "You reminded me that I like to have fun."

"Everybody likes to have fun."

"Yeah, but some of us need to learn how to do it." Kristen had brought him into her family. Nina had eased him into her social circle.

She smiled. "Well, you caught on really quickly."

His chest pinched with a pleasure-pain. This was why he liked her. And what made her different from Nina. Kristen didn't flirt. She didn't have to flirt to make him feel good about himself, or life, or her. All she had to do was make him feel normal, worthy, honorable…and she did that by being herself, letting him be himself.

So though there were similarities between her and Nina; there were also differences. Big differences. "I like having fun."

"But…?"

"No but. Just a statement." He blamed Jason's

stupid comment for the fact that he was fumbling for what he really wanted to say. That she was warm. That she was honest. That she was everything he wanted.

The music stopped and they drifted out of their dance hold, but he didn't let go of her hand. He needed to take her somewhere out of the ballroom. Somewhere they could talk. As he glanced around for a doorway that might lead to a private alcove, there was a commotion at the entry, and then King Mason strode to the stage, carrying a baby.

He took the microphone. "For those who don't know, this is James Tiberius Sancho." He kissed the little boy's cheek. "He's my daughter's nephew by marriage. Dom and Ginny Sancho's son."

Dark haired, dark eyed, the child was as cute as a kid could be. The people clustered around the stage testified to that with their "Aw, isn't he cute," and "What a beautiful little boy."

Dom and Ginny stood only a few feet away, proud, beaming parents, with Ginny's mom and Dom's dad, the King and Queen of Xaviera, now also married, looking on like the happiest grand-parents in the world.

Kristen laughed. "That kid is going to be one spoiled child."

Dean slid a glance to her. "Yeah, well, he *is* going to be a king someday."

"His parents will make sure he's raised right," Kristen said with authority. "Dom looks all cool and sophisticated, but he's got a father's heart."

A father's heart.

Dean's throat tightened. He had absolutely no idea what that was. Nina might have been able to ease him into her social group, and Kristen might be able to ease him into her family, but no amount of "easing" could make up for the shortcomings that counted.

Kristen tugged on his hand. "Come on. Let's go say good-night."

Dean tugged her back. "To a baby?"

"Sure. He's a sweetie. I've met him a few times when Dom and Ginny visited Eva and Alex."

She tugged again.

He tugged her back again. "But there's so much family around him already."

Kristen laughed. "That's the way they like it. The Sancho men were alone for so long that they love being surrounded by people. They especially love showing off Jimmy." She smiled. "Come on."

He almost took a step. Almost. But something held him back. From the corner of his eye, he saw Jason approaching.

Relief rippled through him when Jason said, "What's going on?"

Kristen said, "We were just going to say goodnight to Jimmy."

Jason laughed. "Cutest kid I've ever seen. But Dean and I really need to talk about a thing. So why don't you go and we'll catch up later."

He saw Kristen hesitate. Inside him, a small battle ensued. He wanted to go with her. He wanted to take this step. But he couldn't and he thanked the heavens Jason needed to talk to him.

Kristen walked away and Dean turned to Jason. "So what do we need to talk about?"

"Nothing." He laughed. "I could just see that you needed rescuing."

"That obvious?"

"Nah. I just know you. Kids freak you out."

Dean stuffed his hands in his trouser pockets. "Yeah, well, I'm going to have to get over it." He nudged his head in Kristen's direction. "I really like her."

Jason snorted. "Of course you do. She's gorgeous. And just like with Nina, you're in love in two weeks." He batted his hand. "You're so predictable with a certain kind of woman. You like them strong and smart. But it almost seems that subconsciously you pick somebody you really can't have. Nina was already taken, and this one—" He pointed at Kristen. "Is moving on."

Confused, Dean faced Jason again.

"You didn't hear that the royal family gave her the boot today?"

"What? They fired her?"

"No. No. They gave her the 'shove the bird out of the nest' dismissal. Rumor has it they also contributed to the tune of a million dollars."

Pleasure for her shimmied through him. "That's great."

"It's fantastic. For her. And who got her to this point? You. You introduced her to Mrs. Flannigan. Just like you gave Nina the way to get to Alex, you gave Kristen the way to get to know the people who could set her on the right course."

Dean's blood ran cold. "Are you saying she used me?"

"I don't think she did it deliberately. I don't think she realized the kind of clout that you have, but the genie's out of the bottle now. She's gotten her introductions and literally millions of dollars of funding. She doesn't need you anymore. And you still have weeks of work on a failing project."

Dean stood frozen, trying to link the things Jason said to Kristen's behavior and he just couldn't do it. True, he and Kristen were in two different places with their careers. But there was no law that said they had to be in the same place.

He wanted to support her. He wanted her to support him. "She's exactly where she needs to be."

"And so are you."

Dean frowned. "Excuse me?"

Jason took Dean's shoulders and turned him to face Kristen, who stood by King Mason, playing peekaboo with Jimmy. "Look at her, Dean. She is in her element. She is going to travel around the world and build schools. And what she needs is some big blond guy name Sven to hold down a fort at home. Maybe run the family farm. So that when she comes home, she will see her beautiful, well-adjusted babies and rest up before she has to go to Africa or Asia or South America."

"That's ridiculous."

"What's ridiculous? You don't think she deserves a nice home, the family she wants?" He waved a hand. "Forget it. Forget I said anything. You want to mess with the life of a woman who's finally got her act together, who deserves to have the family she wants, who worked damned hard to get there, then who am I to stop you? Just remember you were in a car behind Nina, chasing her down, refusing to take her no for an answer when she jumped into that boat. You might have been cleared of any wrongdoing, but you're in no way an innocent."

As Jason said the words, Kristen approached, her smile broad, her eyes gleaming.

Jason said, "You should be mingling with your staff, making them feel welcome."

Jason's assertion that Dean was to blame for Nina's death was like a knife in Dean's heart. He hadn't been chasing her. True, he'd followed her from the restaurant, but once he realized she was going to the marina, he pulled together his pride and turned around. He'd been cleared of wrongdoing because Nina had driven five miles knowing he wasn't chasing her.

The fact that Jason would bring it up—would make him remember—put a chill in his blood again.

"The staff is fine."

Jason shrugged. "Okay. Whatever. If you want to lose what you have I'm not going to take the blame."

Jason shifted away about the same time Kristen reached Dean. He felt the rush of happiness that she was near, but Jason's comments rang in his ears. His company had teetered on the brink of failure for months after Nina's death.

And now here he was with Kristen. A woman on the edge of having everything she wanted. It infuriated Dean that Jason would connect Kristen and Nina, and, worse, suggest that he would ruin Kristen's life.

Because he could? Because that's who he was? Or because Jason knew, just as Dean knew, that his upbringing didn't lend itself to Dean being the most understanding, most easy-to-live-with guy in the world.

She said, "That baby's a doll."

Everything about her seemed to glow. And he suddenly saw what Jason saw. Not a comparison between her and Nina, but a comparison between *himself* and Kristen. Kristen was right now as he had been when he met Nina. She looked strong, but looks could be deceiving. Inside of everyone taking their first shaky steps was the potential to screw up royally.

As he had with Nina.

Jason wasn't worried that Kristen was using him. He was worried that if Dean hurt Kristen, she'd spiral out of control as he had after Nina's death…and she'd lose her dream.

She caught his hand, as naturally, as perfectly,

as if they belonged together, and crazy fear raced through Dean.

What if he hurt her?

What if something he said or did ultimately hurt her enough to destroy her dream?

Some people really did only get one shot at life.

What if he ruined hers?

"So Dom and Ginny took the baby to their room. They'll leave him with a nanny and be back, but I think it's so cute that they are hands-on parents."

He did too. He imagined that being raised by a nanny could be as cold and unhappy as being raised by a grandmother who didn't want you.

So he couldn't even think he'd work out his fears of being a bad father by hiring help. Help wasn't what a kid wanted or needed. Love was. Love from a parent.

His blood ran cold at the truth of it. He slid his hand out of Kristen's.

"I…um…need to mingle with my staff."

Her smiled grew. "Great. I'd love to meet them."

He took another step back. "No. I'm fine. You mingle with your potential benefactors."

"I've already mingled. I talked with everyone in the receiving line." She grinned. "Any more talk and I'm going to look obnoxious."

She could never look, act or be obnoxious. She was too honest. Too open. And he was nowhere near that.

He was grouchy, lonely, driven. And two weeks in her company couldn't change that. Just as two weeks in her company couldn't possibly cause them to fall in love.

He took another step back. "I don't want you to come with me."

Her eyes brimmed with confusion. "What?"

"Look, I get it that you're excited. I get it that things are going your way. But this is my company, my legacy. I don't want or need your help."

He let the words fall out, deliberately cruel, to chase her away, but also to remind her that she didn't really know him. And getting to know him would be stupid because, in the end, she wouldn't like the person she would find.

He took another step back. "Goodbye, Kristen."

He said it the same way he had the night he'd first kissed her, intending it to be the last time he saw her. Except this time, it wasn't an easy decision. This time he knew her enough to recognize what he was giving up.

He took one last look at her face, one last long glance into her pretty green eyes, and walked away.

CHAPTER FOURTEEN

THE REST OF the reception was a whirlwind for Kristen. Though she'd told Dean she didn't want to make a nuisance of herself with potential benefactors, everybody seemed interested in her cause. Everybody had advice. Start a blog. Do a Kickstarter campaign. Get on Facebook.

By the time she was free enough to look for Dean, he had gone.

She didn't understand what had happened. One minute everything between them was perfect. Warm. Romantic. But also casual, like two people so in tune they didn't have to work at getting along. And the next he was running away from her.

Telling herself not to make a big deal of it, she went home that night, took off her pretty pink gown and fell into a restless sleep. The next morning, she went to the hotel to see him, but he was already working. When she stopped by the meeting room, he had Jason tell her that he was too busy to be interrupted.

"We're at a pivotal moment," he said, smiling patiently. "I finally got him working with staff. *He* told me that there were to be no interruptions." He peered at her over his glasses. "From anyone." He smiled benignly. "It's best that you don't come back. He's a busy man, who really doesn't date. Now that he's made up with the royal family, he'll be dealing with them."

Her heart about pounded itself out of her chest. If it hadn't been for their dance the night before, she might—*might*—have wondered if he hadn't used her to pave the way to make up with Prince Alex.

But that was absurd.

Wasn't it?

She hadn't done anything to facilitate him talking to Eva and Alex—

Except bring him to Grennady.

And tell the princess he was in Grennady two days before they returned home so that Eva had time to get Alex acclimated…

So that by the time they did meet, both Alex and Dean were in a good enough frame of mind to make amends rather than sling accusations.

The truth of it settled in on her, made her breath shiver and her heart hurt.

Once again, she'd been taken in by somebody who used her.

And like an idiot, she'd fallen in love with him.

Except all she had was Jason's word that he didn't want her around.

So that night, she waited until she knew Dean had gone back to his suite. Standing in a quiet corner of the hotel lobby, she watched as he stepped into the elevator for the penthouse. Then she used the house phone to call him. He answered on the second ring.

"Hello?"

"Hey, it's me, Kristen. I stopped by to see you before but Jason said you were busy."

"We're on the verge of being ready to ship the games to beta testers."

"That's great."

"So you can understand why we don't want

any interruptions. I appreciate everything you did for me with Alex and Princess Eva, but we have work to do now."

He hung up the phone and Kristen just stared at the receiver in her hand shell-shocked.

He really had used her.

It had physically hurt Dean to disconnect the call. But he knew this was for her own good. He deliberately led her down a path where she'd draw some wrong conclusions about him and his intentions, to prevent her from trying to get back into his life.

She was a good person and he was a bad bet.

But every day it hurt a little more. Christmas decorations once again looked tarnished. Taunting. He didn't want to hear Christmas music. Didn't want to eat Christmas cookies. Didn't want to see even one Christmas tree. He might be busy, but he was also alone, empty. And he felt the way he had when he was six or eight or even ten. The world around him was celebrating, happy. And he was alone.

Within a few days the bugs in the games were

nearly gone. They tested and retested, found new bugs and fixed them, and by Christmas Eve morning, they were done.

He gave the staff the option of going home for Christmas but everyone unanimously said no. They wanted to spend Christmas in the winter paradise they'd grown to love.

Dean almost took the plane back to New York, but the smart businessman in him couldn't miss the Christmas Eve ball being thrown by the royal family. Grennady had brought his staff back to life. Grennady had saved his company. As a thank-you, he'd made an informal agreement with Princess Eva to bring his staff to Grennady two times a year for corporate retreats. Though it wasn't the commitment she had hoped for, it had given her the idea to entice other tech companies to do the same. He would not be so rude as to walk out on celebrating with the royal family who—in spite of all odds—had become an asset to him.

But he also couldn't stay in the penthouse an entire afternoon, waiting for the hands of the clock to move far enough that he could dress for the ball. So he put on his parka, caught the bus to the resort and snowboarded until his feet were tired and his nose was frozen.

He found new trails, bypassing the ordinary routes usually taken by tourists and suddenly found himself in the most pristine, peaceful valley he'd ever seen.

He reverently swooshed down a small slope to the center so he could take it all in, the mountains, the blue sky, the silence, but when he slid down the final hill, he realized he wasn't alone.

Prince Alex stood staring at the mountains.

He turned to go, but Alex said, "I hear you back there. This isn't my personal mountain. You're welcome to stay."

Dean winced. "Are you sure?"

Obviously recognizing Dean's voice, Alex turned to face him. "It's you."

Alex might have forgiven Dean, his country might have made an alliance with Dean's company, but he'd also told Dean they'd never be friends.

Which Dean totally understood. He quickly said, "You stay. I'll go."

But Alex shook his head. "No. As I said at dinner the night you came to the palace, we can't avoid each other." He laughed. "Especially not now when you've made agreements with my wife."

Dean took one foot off his board and used it to flip it off the ground and into his hands.

Alex frowned. "Still a pro I see."

"It was kind of like riding a bike."

"Good."

"Yes, thank you."

The world became eerily quiet. It was odd seeing Alex in a parka rather than a dark suit or a tux. Dean said, "This is a far cry from the Mediterranean."

Alex gazed around at the wall of mountain on the horizon. "Yes. It is. But it's beautiful here. In a lot of ways, Grennady feels more like home to me than Xaviera."

"Princess Eva is a wonderful person."

"Most of the people in Grennady are wonderful. They're kind. Loyal. Fiercely protective of their own."

"Why do I get the feeling you're trying to tell me something?"

"Because Eva and I are worried that you're going to hurt Kristen."

Dean winced. "You don't have to worry about Kristen. I scared her off at the reception last week."

Alex took a cautious step toward him. "You did?"

Dean shook his head. "I shouldn't tell you this, but it's easy to see Kristen's the kind of woman who wants everything. Not just a career but kids. A family. I'm not that guy."

Alex frowned. "You don't want a family?"

He did. He desperately did. After two visits with Kristen, her brother and her parents, he wanted a real home, real Christmases, a wife to share his dreams, kids to give his life warmth and meaning…

Dean raised his hands. "What difference does it make? She wants something I can't give her."

"You can't have children?"

"No." He shook his head. "It's not that. I didn't have much of a childhood."

"Being a genius?"

"And being raised by someone who was tired. I had no father. No male influences. And my work takes up most of my time. Kristen deserves somebody named Sven who will be what she needs."

"So you scared her off?"

He shrugged.

"Well, this explains why she's barely spoken this week."

Dean's heart thumped. "You've seen her?"

"We tried to set up two meetings but she wouldn't come. Said she was busy with Christmas prep with her mom and we accepted that." Alex's eyes narrowed. "But that wasn't it. She was probably at home licking her wounds."

Dean said, "I'm sorry."

"Really?"

"Of course. I love her. Everything about her. But she deserves better."

Alex put his hands on his hips and sighed heavily as he looked at the sky for a few seconds. "You are a crazy weird man, Dean Suminski. I shouldn't help you but I'm going to."

"Help me?"

He took a long breath, glanced at the mountains, then looked at Dean again. "It doesn't matter if you think you're made to have kids or not, marriage material or not. If you've found someone who makes you want all those things, then you don't let the chance go by."

Alex shifted his ski poles. "You work things out. You talk about things. And in the end, everything comes together."

Hating that assessment, Dean scoffed. "Like destiny? Or maybe magic?"

Alex laughed, pushed his goggles over his eyes. "It isn't magic. It's work." Using his poles he swooshed himself down the slope, then stopped and in a spray of snow faced Dean again. "It's a lot of work," he called up the mountain. "But it's worth it. Don't let your chance pass you by. Because if you really love her, and I think you do, you're going to regret it."

Kristen had all but decided not to go to the royal family's Christmas Eve party when her mom appeared in her room. "You're not dressed."

Kristen sat up on her bed, saw her mom in a bright red Christmas gown and her eyebrows rose. "You are dressed. What's up?"

"Your dad and I were invited to this year's Christmas party too."

"Really?"

"Something about my position with you in your charity." She sat on the bed and nudged Kristen's shoulder. "Thanks for putting your mom on your board."

Kristen laughed. "You're one of the smartest people I know. You might not be able to make a million-dollar contribution, but I think we need you."

"So, since I'm such a smart person, I'm going to give you a piece of advice."

"I'm not going to the party."

"I know you don't want to see Dean, but your days of cocooning yourself in here because you're upset over a guy dumping you are done. You don't have that luxury. You need to go to this party." She rose from the bed. "Even if you go late, you need to go. If nothing else, you need to show your benefactors that in spite of being upset you will do your job."

Kristen sighed.

Her mother headed out the door. "Your dad and I are leaving now. We don't want to miss a minute. I'd thought we'd all ride together but we don't want to wait for you to dress."

She laughed as her mom disappeared from sight, but when she was gone, she squeezed her eyes shut. Her mother was right. She needed to put in an appearance. She needed to look strong and happy because her charity was coming together. She couldn't let losing one man, one man who had used her, cause her to crumble.

She had to be strong.

Unfortunately, because she'd convinced herself it was okay to stay home, she hadn't shopped that week and she had nothing to wear.

She suddenly missed Stella.

Then she saw the black gown hanging in the back of her closet. Memories of how fun that party had been caused her heart to stutter and she almost decided she couldn't do this. She couldn't see Dean. She couldn't face the fact that he'd used her.

But as quickly as she thought that, she realized she had to see Dean. She had to prove to herself, to him and to everybody that nothing would keep her from doing her duty for her charity.

A quick trip through the receiving line at the royal family's Christmas Eve party gained Dean entrance to the ballroom. Huge silver and gold ornaments hung from the high ceiling with tinsel that arched between each bell and ball and then looped over to the next. Glittering crystal vases held red rose centerpieces on the round tables. The table for the royal family was awash with twinkling white lights. Replete with the scents of roast goose, good wine and sweet treats, the room smelled like heaven.

Dean saw every style and color of gown, glittering necklaces and every hairdo from simple to fancy. But he didn't seen Kristen, and he wondered, as Alex had said, if he hadn't let his chance pass him by.

He'd thought through everything Alex had said and knew he was right. Dean did love Kristen. He was afraid. But he'd spent most of his childhood alone, then ten years unable to trust, and he couldn't do that anymore. He wanted everything Kristen had to offer.

When he still hadn't seen her at dinner, he glanced at the entry one more time, worried that he'd hurt her enough that she'd decided to miss this ball. King Mason had made a Christmas toast. Dancing had begun. She'd be here by now, even if she only intended to put in an appearance for her royal family's sake.

When he saw her parents mingling without her, his breath stuttered and the truth settled in. She wasn't coming.

Jason walked up to him with two flutes of champagne. "Here. We need to toast."

"Toast?"

"Our success today. With that game going to beta testers a week early, I think we proved we're everything we said we were."

Dean laughed in spite of himself. "I guess we did."

"I thought I'd lost you to the pretty blonde, but in the end you came back stronger, if that's possible."

Dean's brow furrowed. "Wait. What?"

"You and Kristen. The thing between you was pulling you away. I had to put a wedge between you."

Dean just stared at him for a second. "First, you didn't put a wedge between us. You said some things that made me realize I might not be good for her. But in the end it was my choice." Not that he was proud of it, but he didn't like the idea that Jason seemed to think he controlled him. "Second, if you ever do anything like that again, you'll be fired so fast your head will spin." Even as he said that, he wondered what he was still doing at this party. He handed the champagne glass back to Jason. "Now, I'm going to go find her and fix this."

Oddly, Jason trying to take credit for breaking him and Kristen up only made Dean stronger. Maybe he'd needed to think through everything he had in the past week before he could make a real commitment. Maybe he'd needed to run back to his fortress of work to realize it was a cold, empty place without the woman he loved. Whatever the reason, he was back now. Stronger. Smarter. He would win her back.

Just when he was ready to get his coat and call a cab to go to the Anderson farmhouse, the ballroom doors opened and Dean's head snapped toward them.

Wearing the black dress she'd worn in New York, the one Dean had bought her, Kristen stepped into the ballroom. All the feelings from that night came tumbling back to Dean. How she'd fit with his crowd of friends. How she'd relaxed him enough that he could mingle and enjoy the party he'd been dreading. How he'd known from the second he'd taken her into his arms to dance with her that she was his other half. The woman of his dreams. His perfect partner.

He didn't let two seconds pass. He raced over to her. "Kristen."

She turned slowly but didn't say anything. Her green eyes caught his gaze. But there was no sparkle in them. No warmth for him. No welcome.

"I'm sorry."

"Sorry things didn't turn out better for you? I can't imagine how since you seem to have gotten everything you want. Your game went to the beta testers today. A week ahead of schedule. Rumor has it you're not worried about a new set of comments because this time the team got it right. You don't have to move to Grennady... Though you have a free pass to return for corporate retreats anytime you want. You have access to our labor pool. You're basically giving us nothing and getting everything...and all it took was making a fool of me to get it." She raised her chin. Her dull green eyes filled with hurt. "If you'll excuse me."

She took a step away from him but he caught her hand. "I know this looks bad."

She laughed. "Looks bad?" She shook her head as if his audacity amazed her. "Get lost."

She wrangled her hand out of his and slid into the crowd. Sidling up to an American couple, she accepted their warm greeting and began to talk animatedly, probably about her charity.

Remorse tightened his chest. Not that she didn't need him, but that he'd needed time to think this through, to realize not just what he wanted but that he could be what Kristen wanted. In the moment, he'd felt he was being noble. Now he realized he hadn't had the right to make the decision to end their relationship by himself.

And even if he couldn't win her back, he couldn't let her go through life thinking any part of this was her fault.

He marched over to her. "Excuse me," he said to the Americans, who smiled politely. "But Kristen owes me this dance."

She said, "I don't—"

But he didn't give her a chance to finish. He tugged her along to the dance floor where he took her into his arms.

"I'm not just sorry that I treated you badly after the reception. I love you."

The words hung in the air as Kristen stared at him and little things settled into his brain.

Like the way she felt in his arms and the way he felt in general. He wasn't playing a role. He wasn't doing what was expected. He was simply being himself.

And that was why he loved her. She wasn't just wonderful. She was the one person with whom he could be himself. His real self. The person he longed to be.

Kristen saw the second he realized what he'd said. Though part of her wanted to yank her way out of his arms and leave him, the other part melted. She knew how huge this was for him.

Unfortunately, he'd also hurt her and he would hurt her again if she let him.

She couldn't let him.

"My whole point in walking away was to save you from getting hurt."

"Too late for that."

"I hurt myself as much. But not for the reasons you think. It hurt me to know you were hurting. And that sort of messed up my whole plan."

Curiosity overwhelmed her and her gaze met

his. His brown eyes were soft, almost happy. She wanted to deck him.

"In trying not to hurt you I hurt you."

"You don't need to spell it out. I got it."

And she was softening again, mellowing to him. Not because he deserved her kindness, but because there was something about him that meshed with something in her. If either one of them believed in destiny anymore, she'd think they were cursed. As it was, she wondered if her hormones weren't out of whack to make her believe she belonged with this crazy man.

"You see, I thought that the fact that I can't be a good dad would either keep us from having kids or mess up our lives if we did have kids."

She almost stopped dancing. "What?"

"I meant what I said about loving you. And loving you meant that I wanted everything you did…even kids."

She did stop dancing. "And you saw far enough ahead to worry about what would happen if we had kids?"

He nodded.

"You didn't stop to think you could look up fatherhood on YouTube?"

To her surprise, he burst out laughing. "Never thought of it. The idea of having a child or two or three paralyzed me and all I could think was how unfair that was to you." He sucked in a breath. "But there's more."

The music stopped. Some couples left the floor. New couples meandered on.

He took her hands. "You're at the start of your life, a wonderful career. I worried that I would drag you down."

His hands holding hers felt so right, so good, but she couldn't let herself give in. If they had a relationship, they had to be equals.

She carefully said, "You don't seem worried now."

"Because I finally realized I wouldn't hold you back. In some ways knowing me might actually help you." He grinned. "I did introduce you to Mrs. Flannigan."

A laugh bubbled up. She raised her eyes to his. "So you love me?"

He rubbed his chest. "A lot, if the pain in my heart is any indicator."

She stepped close. The music started again. Couples waltzed around them, but they didn't move. "Love is actually a very happy thing."

He snorted. "I'd never have guessed."

She laid her hands on his chest, flattened them against his silk shirt. "I have so much to teach you, grasshopper."

He laughed.

She let her hands slide up to his shoulders.

His soft brown eyes caught hers. "You don't hate me?"

"I love you. But we're going to have to make a pact. You don't get to make decisions for me. We talk about things."

He smiled. "Okay."

Her hands finally met at his nape. "Okay."

A second went by, then two. "You could kiss me now."

He laughed, dipped his head, pressed his lips to hers and Kristen's heart sang. The love of her life was a strong, opinionated, sometimes arrogant man, but she had no doubt she was his equal.

He broke the kiss. Couples danced around them. He shoved his hand in his jacket pocket. "We need a little something to seal this deal." He pulled his hand out and dropped a diamond bracelet into her hand.

She gasped. "My bracelet!"

"Aha! I knew you liked it!"

She bounced to her tiptoes and kissed him. "Of course I liked it. I just didn't want to take such an elaborate gift from someone I didn't know."

"You think you know me?"

"Oh, I think we're going to spend the rest of our lives getting to know each other." She rose to her tiptoes to kiss him again. "But that's what's going to make our lives interesting and fun."

He took her hand, led her off the dance floor, and Kristen nestled against him. They hadn't had the most conventional courtship, but once-in-a-lifetime love had nothing to do with normal, ordinary things.

She had no doubt she and Dean Suminski would change the world…

Because together they were stronger than they were alone.

* * * * *

MILLS & BOON®
Large Print – February 2017

The Return of the Di Sione Wife
Caitlin Crews

Baby of His Revenge
Jennie Lucas

The Spaniard's Pregnant Bride
Maisey Yates

A Cinderella for the Greek
Julia James

Married for the Tycoon's Empire
Abby Green

Indebted to Moreno
Kate Walker

A Deal with Alejandro
Maya Blake

A Mistletoe Kiss with the Boss
Susan Meier

A Countess for Christmas
Christy McKellen

Her Festive Baby Bombshell
Jennifer Faye

The Unexpected Holiday Gift
Sophie Pembroke

0117 Rom LP

MILLS & BOON®
Large Print – March 2017

Di Sione's Virgin Mistress
Sharon Kendrick

Snowbound with His Innocent Temptation
Cathy Williams

The Italian's Christmas Child
Lynne Graham

A Diamond for Del Rio's Housekeeper
Susan Stephens

Claiming His Christmas Consequence
Michelle Smart

One Night with Gael
Maya Blake

Married for the Italian's Heir
Rachael Thomas

Christmas Baby for the Princess
Barbara Wallace

Greek Tycoon's Mistletoe Proposal
Kandy Shepherd

The Billionaire's Prize
Rebecca Winters

The Earl's Snow-Kissed Proposal
Nina Milne

MILLS & BOON®

Why shop at millsandboon.co.uk?

Each year, thousands of romance readers find their perfect read at millsandboon.co.uk. That's because we're passionate about bringing you the very best romantic fiction. Here are some of the advantages of shopping at www.millsandboon.co.uk:

* **Get new books first**—you'll be able to buy your favourite books one month before they hit the shops

* **Get exclusive discounts**—you'll also be able to buy our specially created monthly collections, with up to 50% off the RRP

* **Find your favourite authors**—latest news, interviews and new releases for all your favourite authors and series on our website, plus ideas for what to try next

* **Join in**—once you've bought your favourite books, don't forget to register with us to rate, review and join in the discussions

Visit **www.millsandboon.co.uk**
for all this and more today!